A PERFECT MISTAKE

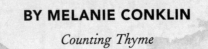

BY MELANIE CONKLIN

Counting Thyme

Every Missing Piece

A PERFECT MISTAKE

MELANIE CONKLIN

LB

LITTLE, BROWN AND COMPANY

NEW YORK BOSTON

Little, Brown and Company
Hachette Book Group
1290 Avenue of the Americas, New York, NY 10104
Visit us at LBYR.com

First Edition: July 2022

Little, Brown and Company is a division of Hachette Book Group, Inc. The Little, Brown name and logo are trademarks of Hachette Book Group, Inc.

The publisher is not responsible for websites (or their content) that are not owned by the publisher.

Watercolor mountains on title page © Pisarenko Olga/Shutterstock.com; notebook vector © alya_haciyeva/Shutterstock.com; pine forest vector © grop/Shutterstock.com; winking line smiley © Ammnezia/Shutterstock.com.

Library of Congress Cataloging-in-Publication Data
Names: Conklin, Melanie, author.
Title: A perfect mistake / Melanie Conklin.
Description: First edition. | New York : Little, Brown and Company, 2022. |
Audience: Ages 8–12. | Summary: Eleven-year-old Max struggles with his ADHD and making mistakes, so when a mistake leaves one friend in a coma and another shutting him out, Max resolves to find out what really happened that night.
Identifiers: LCCN 2021040266 | ISBN 9780316668583 (hardcover) |
ISBN 9780316668606 (ebook)
Subjects: LCSH: Attention-deficit hyperactivity disorder—Juvenile fiction. |
Best friends—Juvenile fiction. | Friendship—Juvenile fiction. | Guilt—
Juvenile fiction. | Detective and mystery stories. | CYAC: Attention-deficit hyperactivity disorder—Fiction. | Best friends—Fiction. | Friendship—
Fiction. | Guilt—Fiction. | Detective and mystery stories. |
LCGFT: Detective and mystery fiction.
Classification: LCC PZ7.1.C646 Pe 2022 | DDC 813.6 [Fic]—dc23/eng/20211004
LC record available at https://lccn.loc.gov/2021040266

ISBNs: 978-0-316-66858-3 (hardcover), 978-0-316-66860-6 (ebook)

Printed in the United States of America

LSC-C

Printing 1, 2022

FOR MY BOYS,
WHO NEVER SIT STILL

1

DEAR MAX

IT'S THE FIRST DAY of sixth grade and I'm writing a letter to my future self. Ms. Little, my sixth-grade English teacher, says she does this every year. You write what you hope to accomplish at the beginning of the year, and on the last day of school, she mails the letters.

That way we can see how much we've grown.

Honestly, I hope I won't have grown at all. I'm almost six feet tall, and it's the worst. People always think I'm in high school, or that I shouldn't be hanging out with the "little kids." One time, this old lady at the grocery store even thought I was someone else's *dad*.

Across the room, Joey's hunched over his tablet, not looking at me. This is the first time I've seen him since the hospital. Since the night Will got hurt.

Joey won't talk to me or answer any of my texts, and I have no idea why. He's sitting with Cam Montgomery and Elijah Watts, acting like me and Will never existed. Like we didn't spend the whole summer planning how we were going to start middle school together. Max, Joey, and Will. The Three Broskateers.

Cam laughs. He's got something—a folded piece of paper that Joey marks and passes on. Seat by seat, the paper makes its way to Samantha Bovella, who's sitting next to me. She glances at whatever's written on the paper and closes it without writing anything. She tries to hand it back to the kid on her other side. When that kid won't take it, Samantha slips the paper under the edge of my binder. It sits there like a bomb waiting to go off.

The smart move would be throwing it away without looking, but I can't do that.

I pick up the paper. Unfold it. My throat tightens.

Do you think the big kid flunked? Yes or No.

The *Yes* column is covered in tallies. More tallies than there are even kids in this class. There's one lonely mark under *No*, but one against a hundred is nothing.

I hunch a little lower in my seat and try to act like I don't care, even though I feel like I'm wearing a clown suit. I don't know most of these kids. We went to different elementary schools. They don't know anything about me, either, other than what they see.

I'm tall. Taller than all the other kids in sixth grade. Some of the teachers, too.

When I walked into the classroom, I sat down as fast as I could, but the other kids still stared. Now they're making fun of me, saying I must have failed a grade, and Joey's not doing a thing to stop it. He's just staring at his tablet like we were never friends at all.

I know what's coming the rest of the day, too.

Questions like:

How old are you?

How's the weather up there?

Are you on the basketball team?

Ms. Little calls for attention and repeats the directions for the letter, which reminds me I'm supposed to be writing mine. She has all these words written on the board: *hero, sibling, dreamer, dancer.* We're supposed to use key words to describe ourselves and connect them to what we want to accomplish by the end of the year, but that's not as easy as it sounds. There are words I could use to describe myself: *ADHD, gamer, tall, skinny, white.* But what about all the stuff you can't describe with just one word, like how I can understand most things, but I don't always get the best grades? Or how I have this magical ability to mess up everything I touch? Last year, I got the Bermuda Triangle Award for "most homework gone missing." My teacher was just trying to be funny, but it sucked. Dad says middle school will be better. Mom says I'm fine the way I am. The problem is, I don't know if I like who I am.

"Can I *help* you?" Samantha Bovella says, making me jump.

"What?"

"You're staring at me."

My face goes hot. "No, I wasn't."

"Yes, you were."

"I didn't mean to," I say, and she turns away in disgust.

My ADHD is called inattentive type, which means I zone out a lot. It's not that I can't pay attention. It's that my brain pays attention to everything, all the time. Like the hands spinning on Ms. Little's cat-face clock, and the lights buzzing overhead, and the sickly sweet smell of breakfast from this morning's meal service. Plus, the papers fluttering under the air vent, and Joey laughing with Cam and Elijah, and the cool metal of my fidget ring as I spin it on my finger. It's like having a hundred TVs on all at once. My therapist says this is a superpower, not a deficit, but sometimes it's exhausting. When I get overloaded with too many channels, my brain shuts everything out, which looks a lot like daydreaming to other people.

Or staring at Samantha Bovella's face.

I twirl my pencil and look at my paper. I know what my new teacher wants. She wants me to write about having fun and winning at sports and getting good grades. All the usual things you'd want to accomplish by the end of a school year. That's what my parents want for me, too. But what I want has nothing to do with school. I want to go back in time. I want to change everything that happened last weekend. I want Will to be okay, and Joey to be nice to me again.

I want my friends back.

When Ms. Little gives us a two-minute warning to wrap up our letters, my paper is covered in doodles instead of words. I rush to write something before time is up.

Dear Max,

I hope you figured it out. I hope you found a way.

2
FRENEMIES

I WASN'T ALWAYS THIS tall. Up until last year, I was just a little big for my age. Then the growth spurt hit. By the end of fifth grade, I was head and shoulders above everyone else. I grew four more inches over the summer, which makes me five-ten now. Grown-up size, and I'm only eleven. Everyone expects me to act like a grown-up, too.

Too bad I'm not one.

If I was, maybe people wouldn't be so disappointed in me all the time.

In eighth period, instead of going to my advisory session, I go to see Ms. Chen, the school social worker. Her papers are in neat stacks. Her bangs are a straight line. She clicks her pen open. "It's nice to meet you, Max. I wanted to check in with you regarding Will Schwartz's hospitalization. I'm here to support you however you may need, okay?"

While she's talking, I'm repeating what she's saying in my head, and also thinking about what I have to say, as well as the birds tweeting outside her open window.

I realize she's waiting for me to answer, so I say, "Okay."

"I understand you and Will are very close. How are you feeling?"

"I'm good. I mean, it sucks, but I'm fine, I guess. . . ."

Meanwhile, my palms are sweating. Will's accident wasn't my fault, but I still *feel* like it was. Every time I think about it, my stomach twists.

"How are you sleeping?" Ms. Chen asks.

"Pretty good."

"Any trouble focusing in class?"

I bark out a laugh, and her brow furrows.

"I have ADHD," I say.

"Oh, yes. That's right. I have your 504 form right here. Are you experiencing any additional difficulties?"

I shake my head and she marks something down, then clicks her pen shut. I'm exhausted from paying attention all day. My brain feels like Jell-O.

She offers me a mint while I fight back a yawn.

"Want to play UNO?" she asks.

A wave of energy lifts me up. I love games.

There's this arcade on the way home from school called Yestercades. It's filled with old games that my parents played when they were kids. *PAC-MAN*, *Joust*, and *Q*bert*, but also Skee-Ball and air hockey, plus sodas and snacks. Lots of kids go there after school. Joey does. Will did.

And so did I, until now.

Five days ago, Will and Joey were my best friends.

Now Will's in the hospital and Joey's treating me like I'm dirt.

When I get to the arcade, I slow down, my eyes catching on a group of kids inside. Joey's light blond hair glows in the neon lights. My heart sinks. I've played video games at Yestercades my entire life, but now I can't even go in to check the high scores. Not while Joey's in there, taking up all the space with his new friends. I've known Joey since we were three years old, but he's always been the kind of friend who can turn on you when things aren't going his way. I guess that makes us frenemies.

I can't play right now, anyway. After what happened to

Will, Mom will freak out if I don't get home on time. Here in Oakwood, New Jersey, we walk to and from school every day, unless your parents drive you. Mom offered to drive me today, but I passed. I don't need her crying her eyes out in front of everyone at school right now.

I take a step back and notice a bunch of handwritten signs taped to the arcade's windows.

WE LOVE YOU, WILL!

WE'RE THINKING OF YOU!

GET BETTER SOON!

The words hit me like slaps.

Will's mom's voice echoes in my ears.

What happened to him? What did you do?

This gross, slimy feeling gathers in the pit of my stomach. I'm not the one in the hospital, so I should be okay, but I'm not. None of this is okay.

Joey's head swivels my way.

I scram before he sees me standing there, watching through the window like a loser.

When I get home, it's way later than it should be, and there's this huge van parked in front of our house. It's super long, like someone took a normal van and stretched it. The supervan is grass green with tan stripes and a framed picture of a cat hanging from the rearview mirror.

"Whose van is that?" I ask as I rush through the back door into the kitchen, where my sister Shelley is stationed at our little round breakfast table, surrounded by textbooks.

"Launch pad," she says, without lifting her eyes from her laptop.

I groan and hurry back to the door to drop my bag on the launch pad we set up for school, to help me keep up with my stuff on the way in and out.

"Is that you, Max?" Mom calls. "We're in here."

I grab a banana and peel it as I half jog to the living room, where I find Mom sitting with my uncle, who I haven't seen in years. "Sorry I'm late—"

"Holy smokes!" my uncle shouts. "What have you been feeding this kid, Em? The last time I saw him, he was half this size. How tall are you now, buddy?"

"Five-ten."

"Wow! That's something else." He sits there grinning.

Mom smooths her perfectly neat hair. "Max, you remember your uncle Calvin?"

I do, but not the way she means. My memories take a while to dig up and sometimes they go missing. Mom remembers everything she's ever said or done. Her brain is like a computer, not a bunch of TV channels playing all at once.

"Please, it's Cal." He lifts his hand for a high five. His face is sunburned. Greasy hair peeks out from under his knit cap. His flowered shirt hangs open over a stained white tank top, and instead of shoes, he's wearing cheap yellow flip-flops.

I give him the five and he grins.

"How was your first day of school?" Mom asks.

I take a deep breath. I'm so tired. "It was good."

"You met the social worker?"

"Yep. She's nice."

Mom smiles. "Do you like your teachers so far?"

"Yeah, they're okay."

"That's great, honey. Do you want to go see Will this afternoon?"

Cold slime pours through me.

Mom's still talking. "Gina says they don't need any food for tonight, thanks to the meal train, but I was thinking we could bring them some—"

"I don't want to go to the hospital!" I blurt out. This happens with ADHD. Sometimes I say things before I think, and sometimes I say them too loud.

"That's fine," Mom says. "Are you all right, honey?"

I force a smile. "I'm good. Just tired."

I'm tired of feeling sick every time someone says Will's name, and I'm tired of feeling guilty for not visiting him in the hospital—because Will's not just in the hospital, he's in a medically induced coma, and we won't know for sure if he's okay until they wake him up. All I know is that I let him down and I feel terrible about it.

Uncle Cal takes my silence as his cue. "Tell you what, buddy. How about we crack open a couple of brewskies and shoot the breeze, man to man."

Mom is so shocked her mouth falls open. "Go on, Max," she says, waving me away.

"What?" Cal is all wide-eyed innocence. "I was *kidding*."

Mom glares at him like she's about to commit a murder.

I guess Mom has frenemies, too.

3
THE ROUNDHOUSE

UNCLE CAL SPENDS THE night on the sofa. When I leave for school in the morning, he and Dad are out by the supervan. They've got the rear doors open and are looking at something inside.

"It's an extended passenger van," Cal's saying. "Vintage, from the seventies. Front-wheel drive, full rear suspension, sleeps six. At least it did before I converted it."

Dad's got his hands propped on the edge of the van's roof. At six-five, he's one of the only people who's a whole lot taller than me. He says I'll appreciate my height one day, as if that makes middle school any less horrible right now.

I lean past him to look inside. The van is filled with tools, like the woodshop at the middle school. Long counters line the sides, with cabinets below and pegboard over the windows. Weird-looking machines are bolted to the floor.

"What are the power cords for?" Dad asks, pointing to these orange cables running along the ceiling.

"I've got everything hooked up to a generator," Cal says.

"Wait, I'll show you." He hops into the van and weaves through the mess of machines to the driver's seat. After a few screechy attempts to start, the van's engine roars to life. The exhaust backfires with a bang.

Down the street, the Dog Lady's dogs start barking. Her house is the last one before our street dead-ends. It's the biggest and oldest house in our whole neighborhood, and the lady who lives there has more dogs than I can keep up with. She walks them in the morning and the evening wearing these weird thick-soled shoes, with her hands full of leashes. Big dogs, small dogs, all kinds in one big pack. They bark like crazy whenever there's a loud noise.

"What are all these machines for?" I ask Dad.

He thumps me on the back. "Woodworking. Your uncle's a craftsman, Max."

I watch Cal stumbling back to us in his yellow flip-flops. "Sure he is."

Cal points at a bucket of wood close to me. "Toss me a piece of that molding, bud."

I grab a skinny, rounded stick of wood and hand it over.

Cal flips a switch on one of the machines, and the blade starts moving up and down. The metal whines as it carves into the wood. He switches the machine off.

"Now *that* is a sweet cut," Cal says.

He passes the wood to Dad, who runs his big hands over it and whistles like he isn't as clueless about this stuff as I am. The last time we tried to make something out of wood, my birdhouse looked more like a bird shack.

"Makes me wish I had more time to get my hands dirty," Dad says.

"How's the food science business these days?" Cal asks.

"It's been a while since I had a winner, but this granola pitch is a game changer. I can feel it. I'm happy to have you taste test for me while you're here."

Cal grins. "Anytime, man. The cash fund's a little low, so I gotta see if I can drum up some paying work, but till then I'm all yours. Got anything that needs doing around the house?"

Dad thinks for a few seconds. "Well, there are a few things here and there, but we probably know someone who needs real work done. I'll put the word out."

"Thanks, man." Cal grips Dad's shoulder. "Your dad is aces, Max. You know that?"

Cal smiles his greasy-haired grin while Dad looks at me like he's really seeing me for the first time. "What are you still doing here, Max? You're going to be late for school."

I go to check the time on my phone, but it's not in my pocket. I must have left it inside. It has a million alarms that Mom set up to help me be on time, but they don't work if I forget it.

"I can drive him," Cal offers, but I'm already off and running. This is one of the worst parts of having ADHD. My therapist calls it time blindness. I don't notice time the way other people do. I'm always late to things, unless I set a bunch of alarms or Mom reminds me a million times. I have a hard time planning, too, so I'm horrible at projects. My therapist says I live in the *now*, but I can't be late on the second day of school. This year was going to be different. I was going to use everything we practiced over the summer to do middle school right. But then Will got hurt, and all my plans went sideways.

I careen down the hill into town, cross the main road, and swing around the corner to the middle school. Which is a mistake because I don't see Joey until it's too late.

Somehow, I manage to spin on my size 11 feet and avoid clobbering him.

He jumps back, his eyes wide. He looks small crouched against the building. And scared.

"Hey," I manage. I'm panting hard.

"Hey," he says back.

It's the first thing he's said to me since the hospital.

We stare at each other for a minute.

Then he starts to walk away.

"So, Cam and Elijah, huh?" I call after him.

He turns back. "They live by my mom's apartment. We play basketball together."

"What about soccer?"

He makes a face. "You quit soccer."

He's right. I did. You can only take so many yellow cards before you get the hint that playing against kids half your size is not a good idea.

"Are you mad at me?" I ask.

Joey stubs his sneaker into the sidewalk.

"Dude, come on. It's me."

He glares up at me. "My dad doesn't want me talking to you, okay?"

My neck goes hot. "Why not?"

"That detective called our house again."

"So?"

"So, my dad is mad."

"At me? I didn't do anything!"

"Neither did I!" Joey shouts back. He studies my face for a long minute. "You really didn't say anything else to that detective?"

"I told her the truth. We went to the roundhouse, but I got scared and went home."

What I don't say is that I also told her whose idea it was to go into the woods that night. Because the truth is, I did do something. Joey and I both did.

That part, I remember.

"Come on guys, we have to go," Joey said. "Jared says it's awesome."

"Why's it called a roundhouse?" Will asked, as his go-kart bounced on the screen.

"Because it's round—"

"—and it's a house?" I finished. I launched my player through a shortcut in the race and knocked Will's player off the road. He shouted and shoved me.

Joey leaned in front of the screen, trying to get our attention as we booed. "It's not a house," he said. "No one lives there.

It's this old building in the middle of the Res. They stored trains there a really long time ago. It's round so they could rotate them into place. Jared says they go there all the time to paint graffiti."

That got my attention. "I love graffiti."

"I know," Joey said, the way you say no duh. *"You down?"*

I jumped up. "Let's do it!"

Will stayed on the couch. "I don't know. It's the middle of the night."

"Come on," Joey said. "No one will know."

"Are you sure your brother wants us there?" Will asked. "He said not to bug him. He had that Scream *mask on again."*

"Relax," Joey said. "Jared's cool with it. Luca's going, too."

"What about your dad?" Will said.

Joey shrugged. "He's asleep."

No one said anything about how weird it was that Joey's dad was snoring in his La-Z-Boy recliner with a bunch of empty beer cans instead of playing video games with us like he usually did.

"Please," Joey said. "It's my birthday."

Will flicked his game controller. He was dragging his feet, but he usually did whatever we said. Like the time we wanted to make a bathtub full of slime in Will's bathroom and he ended up grounded for two weeks for using all his mom's flour and staining the bathtub green.

"Imagine you didn't have enough coins," Joey challenged.

"*Imagine you didn't have a dog,*" *Will shot back.*

Joey leaned in. "Imagine your parents got divorced."

"*Harsh,*" *Will whispered, but we all knew Joey had won.*

The video game pinged and blooped in the background.

Yellow coins and red balloons flashed on the screen.

Will looked at me.

"*Come on,*" *I said. "Let's go."*

4

THE HONOR SYSTEM

MS. LITTLE'S CLASSROOM IS weird. Instead of desks, she has love seats, beanbag chairs, and an old-fashioned bathtub with fancy feet that look like bird claws clutching balls. I've always wondered who came up with that design, and why they imagined a bird might carry a ball in its foot. Is it a pearl? An egg? These feet are painted gold so it's hard to tell.

"Welcome to my incubator," Ms. Little said yesterday, when she introduced herself.

Today, she asks us to gather around.

Joey and Cam and Eli pile into the tub. Within seconds all the good seats are taken, so I sit by the window where I won't block anyone's view. Joey laughs at something Eli says, and my heart pinches.

I remember the day Joey told us his parents were getting divorced. The first day of summer vacation. Joey started crying, which made Will cry. Then we were all crying because the idea of Joey's parents splitting up was so big and scary, it took all three of us to hold it.

Watching Joey and Cam and Eli now, that memory feels like it's from another life. I didn't think things would ever change between us, but I was wrong.

Everything's changed.

Joey catches me looking at the bathtub and frowns. I look away. We were late getting to school after our argument, but luckily the front office didn't give us late slips. It's the first week of school, so they're going easy on us. Joey's dad wouldn't care, but my mom sure would.

"Imagine having no friends," I say under my breath, but there's no one to answer me.

"Good morning, everyone," Ms. Little says. "Today we're starting class with *The Day You Begin*, by Jacqueline Woodson." She lifts a picture book for all to see.

There are a few giggles and some *ughs* from Joey and Cam and Eli's bathtub. Ms. Little silences them with a raised eyebrow and starts reading. At first, I think reading a picture book is a goofy idea, plus it's not easy for me to sit and listen. Then I hear the words.

" 'There will be times when you walk into a room and no one there is quite like you.' "

Ms. Little pauses.

The noises die down. She goes on, reading a story about kids who are each different in their own ways—skin color, accents, summer trips, and lives—but what they all have, too, are their unique gifts. The way Ms. Little reads, in a voice that is soft but certain, I want to believe her. She finishes, and there's this brief moment of quiet when it seems like it's possible we could all get along like that, but then Cam throws a wad of paper at Samantha Bovella who glares at him with the power of a thousand suns, and it's over.

"Cameron, I expect you to respect yourself and your classmates," Ms. Little says, and Cam sinks down into the tub. Joey's face reddens as everyone stares at them.

"As a reminder," Ms. Little says, "a student in our community suffered an accident this week and remains in critical condition. If you feel the need to speak to a counselor, Ms. Chen is available for crisis counseling. This is a difficult time for our community and it's important that we support one another. Our thoughts remain with Will Schwartz and his family." She doesn't look at me or Joey when she says this, but I feel eyes on me.

Yesterday, Principal Fleming sent a memo home about

Will's accident and how his synagogue is collecting donations to help his parents. There's a meeting after school today to make paper cranes for Will, too, as though a bunch of badly folded origami can help a kid in a coma.

Thankfully, Ms. Little moves on. "Let's get out our writer's notebooks, please."

We set up these notebooks yesterday. They're supposed to be a place where we can collect our thoughts, share our dreams, and learn together. Which sounds awful. I have a million ideas, but they don't like to line up in order. And when I try to write them down, my sentences hop all over the place and leave out half of what I want to say. My therapist and I have been practicing ADHD coping skills, but I'm never going to be a straight-A student like Shelley. I wish all we did was math and art. Then I'd be golden.

Ms. Little smiles. "To begin our narrative writing unit, I'd like you to describe an intense moment. Not a day or an hour, but a short period lasting no more than a few minutes."

Samantha Bovella's hand shoots up.

"Yes?"

"Can we write about more than one moment?"

"You can write as much as you'd like," Ms. Little says. "Don't be afraid to explore. Minds are like parachutes—they only function when open. Your writer's notebooks will work on the honor system. Notebooks will be turned in for checks every week, but I won't read your words unless you fold down the corner of the page. It's that simple."

"Really?" Cam says.

"We can write whatever we want?" Eli asks.

"Every meaningful contribution will count toward your grade," Ms. Little says, "but that doesn't mean you can write the word *cat* a hundred times in a row."

"What if we list different kinds of cats?" Cam says.

Ms. Little laughs. The buttons on her shirt are tiny enamel cats in different colors. Which makes me wonder if she has cats at home. Maybe she's the kind of person who loves cats but can't have one because she's allergic. Either way, someone with cat buttons has to be nice. And her writing rules sound okay. Maybe this notebook thing won't be so bad after all. Maybe the pages won't be covered in red lines and question marks when I get them back.

"Could you cut that out?" Samantha Bovella says.

My knee's bouncing against the underside of the table. I make it stop, even though it's harder for me to think when I don't let myself fidget. I've been trying to use my fidget ring in class so I don't draw too much extra attention to myself, but it's not easy.

I write two sentences about the time I busted my knee open playing soccer. Then I hear Joey laugh and I'm thinking about how we used to go to soccer practice together every week. And then I'm noticing the air coming through the air-conditioning vent, which is a soft whirr that winds up quickly but then dies down, on and off, like it's breathing. Every once in a while, it rattles. I run my finger over the corner of my writer's notebook, trying to smooth out the wrinkles from where it got smashed in my book bag. Ms. Little's cat-face clock says I have seventeen minutes until second period. At least I only have to be here today. Then I get a four-day weekend because of Rosh Hashanah. In our district, we go back to school the Thursday after Labor Day, but then the Jewish holidays arrive, which means we're off again. It feels like we don't really get started until October. Which is fine by me.

When fifth grade turned into a disaster and we went to see my therapist for the first time, Mom said, "He was doing so well in school. I don't understand why he's failing now." Dr. Williamson explained that it's common for ADHD to go undiagnosed until a student starts to struggle in school.

She said ADHD was genetic and asked if we had any diagnosed family members. Like this pattern was destined to repeat. I remember thinking it was written into me like a computer program or a recipe. ADHD was a part of me and there was nothing I could do about it.

But Dr. Williamson said there *were* things we could do.

There were skills I could learn to manage my ADHD and there were accommodations we could get to make school more reasonable for me. And if that wasn't enough, we could try medication. It made sense. My brain worked differently, so I needed to do things differently. It's like we're all given the same user manual at birth, but a neurotypical manual doesn't work for someone with ADHD. We spent the summer noticing which strategies *did* work for me so I could write my own manual. One that's just right for *me*. It takes a lot of trial and error.

Usually, that's what we talk about in our Friday sessions.

Today is different.

Dr. W has a new poster on her wall. *Rogue One: A Star Wars Story*. My eyes trace the characters, the blue glow that surrounds them, the giant mass of the Death Star looming in the background. She collects movie posters. Plants too. She says those are because people keep giving them to her, and who is she to turn a helpless plant away? There's something relaxing about watering them.

Today she's sitting still, her cane propped against her chair. Her eyes on me. "What's one good thing from the past week?" she asks, because this is our routine.

"I think I like my English teacher this year."

"Good," she says. "That's wonderful to hear. And what's one bad thing?"

There are so many bad things.

I look down at my spinning fidget ring.

"How about we make a bubble map?" she says, reaching for the paper and crayons she keeps on the coffee table between us. I lean over the table and draw a circle with my name in the middle. Then I add all the people in my life like clouds circling a globe. Green lines connect me to the people I feel good about talking to right now, like Dr. W and Will. Red lines are for the people I can't talk to, like Joey and Jared. Everyone else gets a red line and a green line, including Mom and Dad. I've never had this much red on my map before.

"I'm glad you feel safe sharing here," Dr. W says. "You've been through a traumatic experience, Max. It's normal to feel sad or guilty or ashamed. We don't have to talk about Will, but I need to make sure you're getting the support you need to process your feelings. Especially as someone with ADHD, who tends to feel a lot of shame over perceived failures. I know your Mom's been to the hospital quite a bit to visit and to help out. Have you gone to see Will?"

"No."

"Would you like to?"

"I don't know."

The truth is, I don't want to go, but therapy uses the honor system, too.

"You don't have to feel any kind of way about this, Max," Dr. W says, her voice raspy but kind. "What's important is that you let yourself *feel*. How are you feeling right now?"

Cold slime spreads over me, like oily grossness crawling across my skin. All I can think is that Joey and I are the ones who convinced Will to go out that night. He didn't want to do it, but we made him, and he's the one who got hurt.

What happened to him? What did you do?

"Max? When you think about Will—"

"I'm sorry," I blurt out.

"What are you sorry for?"

"We made Will go with us. Joey wanted to go because his brother was going and I wanted to see the graffiti, but Will didn't want to go and we never should have made him. I just . . . I never thought—" My voice catches.

I shut my eyes, but it doesn't help.

"Breathe," Dr. W says, so soft. "In. Out. That's good, Max. Really good."

We breathe together for a long time.

"It's easy to beat yourself up for the choices you made, Max. It's much harder to forgive yourself, but we're going to work on that, okay?"

I nod. With how bad I feel, it's going to take a lot of work.

5
FAVORS

ON SATURDAY MORNING I wake up to the sound of an explosion. Like a firework. Or a gunshot. I stumble downstairs and find Mom in full real estate agent mode: office clothes, pointy shoes, supersmooth hair. "There's bacon," she says, shoving a plate at me as she cranes her neck to look out the window. "What on earth is your father doing out there? I told him I had to leave first thing this morning." I take the bacon to the table and sit down to eat a plate of half-burnt pancakes. Mom tries her best, but when she's doing two things at once, the food always loses.

Shelley's eating her pancakes dry, next to an open textbook. She pokes me in the side while I'm drenching my pancakes in syrup. "I found the Saran Wrap in the refrigerator again."

"I didn't use the Saran Wrap."

"What about that avocado in the fridge?"

Oh. Maybe I did use the Saran Wrap when I got a snack yesterday. I stare at my pancakes and tell myself not to do that again. "What are you studying? School just started."

"The SATs are in two months."

"Then why are you studying now?"

"It's a cumulative effect," she says with a shrug.

I stuff a big bite of pancake in my mouth as she highlights bits and pieces of the page in front of her. It makes a cool pattern that I wish I understood. We used to watch movies and play board games together, but now that Shelley's a junior, all she does is work on school or hang out with her debate club friends. I don't even know what to say to her anymore.

The back door bangs open. Uncle Cal appears. "Hoo doggy, it's hot as blazes out there." He wipes sweat from his forehead and chugs the glass of orange juice Mom had set out for Dad.

She sighs and gets the carton to pour another.

"Ooh, bacon!" Cal says, sliding the bacon plate in front of him. I grab another slice before they disappear like Dad's juice.

"Tim!" Mom shouts out the back door.

A minute later, Dad appears. He's wiping sticky black stuff from his hands with a rag.

"What are you doing?" Mom says. "I told you I needed to leave first thing. I'm showing that huge Victorian over on Cedar Drive today."

"Sorry, Cal was helping me change the oil on the minivan."

"I needed to top up the van anyway," Cal says. He winks. "She drinks oil like water."

Mom shuts her eyes briefly, then lets out a breath. "Fine. Just try not to do too much damage while I'm gone, okay? Max, spend some time with your uncle today, will you?"

"No can do," Cal says. "I got a gig, thanks to Tim here."

Mom turns to Dad, her eyes wide. "You didn't."

"What? I thought it was a good thing," Dad says. "Tony mentioned he needed some work done at the bakery—"

"You went to the *Bovellas*?" Mom says, her voice climbing. She blows out another breath and checks her watch. "Fine. Max, go with your uncle."

The Bovellas run the only real bakery in town. Ms. Bovella is Mom's friend, but Samantha Bovella is definitely not mine. "Why me?"

"Shelley's meeting with her SAT tutor in an hour, and

clearly, your father can't be trusted." Dad blows Mom a kiss, and she swallows back a smile.

"But it's Saturday."

"Max, please."

This is why I hate favors. When someone asks you for a favor, they're usually asking you to do something you really don't want to do. Like Joey asking to swap sandwiches when his dad sends him tuna fish. Or Will asking to borrow my diamond pickax in our favorite computer game. Mom's asking me to lose my weekend screen time. I think she imagines my brain withering like a raisin from playing video games, when in reality I probably couldn't focus much harder.

"You just don't want me gaming all day."

"No, I'm trying to keep your uncle out of trouble."

Cal winks. "A little trouble never hurt anyone."

"You're hardly in a position to say that," Mom says, which makes me wonder what he did. Rob a bank? Commit a murder? Fold his shirt the wrong way?

Mom puts a hand on my shoulder. "Just keep an eye on him for me, please? Maybe we can go see Will tomorrow. We're signed up to bring them dinner."

My stomach twists. Any argument I was about to make dies on my tongue. All I can think is that I'm here like normal while Will is in the hospital. If I hadn't agreed to go to the roundhouse, we never would have gone, and Will never would have gotten hurt. Mom says you can only learn from the past, not change it, but I wish she was wrong sometimes.

Uncle Cal crams a whole pancake into his mouth and hooks his head toward the door. "Come on, bud. Let's hit the road."

The supervan smells like the fireplace after Dad's made one of his epic Eagle Scout fires but forgotten to open the flue. Like wood, smoke, and burning. White beads line the van's seat backs. Gum wrappers and parking tickets litter the floor. I try to shut the glove box to stop the door from banging into my knees, but it's busted. Then I try to roll my window up, but the handle just spins.

"Sorry, they're broken," Uncle Cal says, jiggling his own handle. His window is stuck halfway open. "Do me a favor and keep your hands inside the ride."

"What if it rains?"

He shrugs. "Then my butt gets wet."

"Imagine being a total mess," I mutter to myself.

"What's that?" Cal says.

"Nothing. It's just this game I play with my friends. Or played, I guess."

He's staring at me. Waiting.

"We imagine bad things happening and whoever says the worst thing wins. Like, 'Imagine having no candy money' or 'Imagine your van going off a cliff.' Stuff like that."

"Weird," he says. "I like it."

"You're weird," I blurt out and regret it immediately, but Cal just winks.

"I'm not weird, I'm limited edition." He hits the gas and the supervan lurches away from the curb. It takes two hands to turn the wheel. He drums his fingers, glancing at me. "That's Princess Leia," he says, pointing at the cat picture hanging from the rearview mirror. "Best cat in the entire galaxy, may she rest in peace."

"Cool." I was fine when we were sitting still, but now that we're driving toward the woods, my hands are sweating. "How long are you staying here?"

"I don't know . . . a week, maybe two? A month tops." He laughs. "I'm a wanderer. I never have liked staying in one place for too long."

"Oh." That's probably why he didn't bother to visit the last few years.

Cal turns onto the road that cuts through the Res and my stomach lurches. The Res is short for the Reservation, which is this giant chunk of forest that's been set aside as a nature preserve with trails running through it. It's September, so the trees are still thick with leaves, but I can see glimpses of light brown trails here and there, which makes my heart race. I should be fine. I told the truth. That's all I can do. I keep telling myself that, but it's not working.

We drive past the place where it happened, and I can't look, because if I do, I'll be sick all over Uncle Cal's supervan. I close my eyes and keep them shut until I'm sure we're past the roundhouse. With my eyes closed, I get this feeling like I'm floating outside of my body, and when I open my eyes, I'll be somewhere else entirely. Like on the moon. Or the bottom of the ocean. But when I open my eyes, I'm still in the supervan next to Uncle Cal.

"You okay over there, Stretch?" Cal asks.

"Don't call me that."

"Okay," he says. "Message received." A pause. "If you ever want to talk about anything, I'm happy to lend an ear. I know things have been tough lately, with your friend—"

"I'm fine!"

"Okay, man. Whatever you say."

We drive the rest of the way to Bovella's in silence,

listening to the tools rattle around in the back of the van. When Uncle Cal parks and turns the engine off, I jump out and make a beeline to the bakery. Inside, the smell of yeast and cinnamon greets me. The counter is so packed with customers, I can barely see the glass cases full of pastries and cookies and cakes.

I'm doing a pretty good job of keeping it together until I look behind the counter. There's a teenage boy with Samantha Bovella's same olive skin and dark brown eyes at the register—her brother, Luca. He takes one look at me and says, "What are *you* doing here?" and the sound of his voice takes me right back to that night.

6
BOVELLA'S

"THIS IS A BAD idea," Luca said, as me and Joey and Will barreled down the sidewalk like a pack of puppies, shoving one another and laughing into the night. It was cold out, but I barely even noticed because there was electricity running through my limbs. I felt like I was flying.

Jared laughed. "They're the ones who wanted to come," he said. "Besides, it's my little bro's birthday. Can't say no on his birthday, right?"

Joey grinned super wide.

Luca just shook his head. He and Jared always hung out, but they usually ignored us or made fun of us instead of inviting us to tag along.

We passed the Dog Lady's house and came to the dead end, where our street stops and the trail into the Res begins. Normally, the trail is leafy and green, but in the middle of the night, it was dark and spooky. Jared and Luca hopped the chain slung across the entrance. Joey hurried after them with his tiny flashlight, the kind you can get at the arcade with five hundred tickets. Then Will and me, side-by-side, even though the path isn't really wide enough for that.

"Are you sure they know where it is?" Will asked, as I narrowly avoided decapitation from a branch that sprang out of the shadows.

"Just chill," Joey said.

Up ahead, Jared whooped. "You babies getting scared yet?"

"No way," Joey shouted back at him, and Jared laughed.

As we climbed uphill, my eyes slowly adjusted to the dark, but I still couldn't have told you exactly where I was. I'd walked these woods a million times, but nothing looked familiar. These were just oak trees and raspberry bushes all around me, but in the darkness, they looked like monsters. You might think being tall helps you be less scared of things like this, but it does not. There are just more things for me to run into.

"What's so great about this place, anyway?" Will asked.

"It's got a NO TRESPASSING sign," Joey said.

"Then why are we going there?" Will said.

Joey laughed. "Imagine being scared of a sign."

Will went quiet.

"It's cool, Will." I bumped his shoulder. "It'll be fun."

The path finally leveled out, and for a minute, I knew where I was. Then Jared and Luca turned down a side path, and that's when I realized I couldn't see the house lights anymore. A wrinkle of worry threaded through me. We probably should have left a note at Joey's house. What if we got lost? I hadn't even remembered to bring my phone.

I could have stopped us right there.

I still knew where we were well enough to get back, but I was too busy tripping over my own feet and knocking branches and spiderwebs out of my face to think about turning back.

Finally, about a million years later, a shadowy building loomed out of the darkness. Joey flicked his feeble light over crumbling bricks covered in graffiti of every color.

"Welcome to the roundhouse," Jared said. He made a "woooo" noise at Luca.

Luca frowned. "Let's get this over with. I'm tired."

Jared tried to grab Luca, who dodged him and ducked through an archway in the bricks guarded by bands of rusty, twisted metal. There were no doors. They must have rotted away.

Jared chased after Luca, his voice echoing as he screamed like a ghoul.

"Come on," Joey said, waving for me and Will to follow. He walked through the overgrown weeds to the archway, climbed through the metal bands, and disappeared.

I ducked under them next. Through the doorway, down a slope of loose gravel with rocks sliding beneath my feet, into pitch darkness.

Will came stumbling down behind me and almost face-planted, but I managed to grab his arm and catch him. I couldn't see anything no matter how hard I stared. My heart was racing. I wished I was back in my room, under the quilt Mom made for me—

Jared whooped, and I jumped half out of my skin. My feet and fingers were freezing. Something scurried away in the dark. Were those claws? What else was in there with us?

Joey's flashlight flicked to the ground, which seemed to disappear up ahead. There was some kind of pit over there. A deep, scary pit surrounded by rusty metal railings. I stepped forward to see it better, and the light cut out.

"Joey, where are you?" Will shouted.

A beat passed. My heartbeat pounded in my ears.

The flashlight clicked on right in front of my face. "Rah-hhh!" Jared shouted.

That's when I turned and ran.

"Max!" I blink and Uncle Cal is right in front of me. Close enough to smell his bacon breath.

I jerk away from him, and he raises his hands. "Okay, kiddo. You do you."

Behind him, Luca Bovella is staring a hole through me, his jaw set in a tight line. His shiny lifeguard sunglasses hang from the neckline of his shirt.

"What are you doing here?" he asks again.

"I'm helping my uncle."

"Did Joey say something to you?"

"About what?"

Luca opens his mouth to say something else.

Cal steps between us. "Could you point us in Tony's direction?"

"That's my dad," Luca says. He stares at me for another long second before he points to the swinging door behind the counter. "He's in the back. Through there."

I can feel Luca's eyes on me as we walk past him. I've been to Bovella's a million times, but this is the first time I've ever wished I hadn't come inside. As we pass through the swinging door, I tell myself I'm never coming back here again.

We step into a massive kitchen, where a hairnetted lady is pounding dough on a long wooden table while another lady feeds trays into huge steel ovens. Mr. Bovella looks up from where he's dumping flour into a mixer the size of my bathtub.

"I'll be right back," Cal says. He goes over to introduce himself while I stand there, hoping Luca Bovella isn't going to come through the door and yell at me again. What does he think Joey said to me? I told the police everything I know. We all did. Right?

"Are you stalking me or something?"

I spin around.

Samantha Bovella is sitting on the counter behind me in a white apron covered with chocolate smudges.

"My uncle's doing some work for your dad."

"Okay, not a stalker, then." She tugs her gloves off, reaches into her apron, and pulls out a small spiral-bound notebook. "I have some questions for you. What do you think about the town's proposal to tear down the historic train building in the Reservation?"

"What proposal?"

"The town wants to tear down the roundhouse because of Will Schwartz's accident."

"Oh."

"You think that's okay? What about the historic significance of the building? Shouldn't it be preserved for future generations?" Her pen hovers over her notebook.

"Why are you asking me?"

She tips her head. "As one of the people involved in Will's accident, I'm interested in your opinion. Have you seen him since he got hurt?"

Will's face flashes in my mind. I push it away. "You should talk to your brother."

"I did. Luca said nothing happened at the roundhouse. He said Will left right after you."

Red hot shame floods my body.

That's what Joey said, too. After I ran away, Will tried to follow me. Then he got lost. And hurt. I've tried to remember if I heard footsteps behind me, but I was too busy freaking out at the time. I for sure didn't hear Will calling out for me. I would have stopped if I'd heard that.

Samantha studies me like she's really seeing every part of my face, from my eyebrows to my chin. "We visited Will at the hospital yesterday. He looked so sad, lying there like a dead body."

My stomach clenches.

I focus on my breathing. *In. Out.*

I remember Mom telling me that Will was in a coma, and how it didn't feel real, and the rabbit hole I fell into when I looked up medically induced comas. Keeping a person in a coma allows their brain to heal, but they can't stay in a coma forever. Most medically induced comas are lifted after two weeks, which is in eight days for Will.

"*Hello*, Max?" Samantha says. "Did you hear what I said?"

I didn't. I'm trying not to barf all over her bakery floor.

I have this overwhelming urge to lie down.

Samantha leans in super close, like I'm incapable of following the sound of her voice. "I *said*, I heard Will had water in his lungs."

I drag my gaze from the floor to her face. "Where did you hear that?"

"A journalist never reveals her sources," she says, with another one of those little head tilts. "I just wondered if you knew anything about it."

"I don't." Apparently, I don't know anything about anything.

"Sweird, right?"

"What did you say?"

"Sweird. Super weird."

"You can't just make up words like that."

"Why not? The dictionary didn't pop out of the air fully

formed, you know. *Tween. Spork. Hangry.* Frankenwords are just more meaning with less words."

I think about it for a second. "Like *frenemy*?"

She sighs. "Yes. Like *frenemy*. Why don't you want to talk about Will?"

"Because I messed up!" I practically shout.

Samantha is stunned silent, her mouth hanging open.

Thankfully, Cal chooses this moment to walk back with Samantha's dad.

"This your partner?" Mr. Bovella asks, looking at me.

"My nephew," Cal says. "He's eleven."

"Oh, Max!" Mr. Bovella says. "I didn't recognize you. You're like a full-grown man." He doesn't look thrilled about it, either. "Sam, I need you out front." Samantha blows out a breath of frustration before tucking her notebook away and hopping down from the counter.

After that, I follow Cal and Mr. Bovella around while they talk about the new dessert cases Mr. Bovella wants Cal to build, but I don't hear much of what they say. I keep thinking about how I ran away that night, and how scary it was. That sick feeling builds in my stomach as images flicker through my mind. *Dark sky. Twisted branches. Flashes of light.* A memory is trying to surface, but I can't grab hold of it, no matter how hard I try.

7
THE SNIFF TEST

IN SOME HOUSES, SUNDAY brunch isn't a big deal, but in our house, it's Dad's taste-testing window. He's been working on a new granola mixture, which means we have ten different styles of granola to try this morning. "Number eight is the spiciest," Dad says. "I'd save that one for last."

Cal dumps a spoonful of rosemary granola on his plate. "Savory granola, huh?"

Dad grins. "No one's cornered the market yet."

My mouth tastes like potpourri thanks to Granola Number One. "Maybe there's a reason why."

"Max," Mom says.

"No, it's okay," Dad says. "Finding the right answer is often a process of elimination."

"Ooh, I like the spicy one," Cal says. "Smells great, too. Sweet *and* salty."

Shelley pops a few pieces in her mouth and chokes. "Water," she wheezes.

"Dairy is better to neutralize the heat," Mom says, passing Shelley a glass of milk. Of course, Mom's prepared. Computer brain.

Shelley chugs the milk and shivers. "It's not bad," she says to Dad. "It just went down the wrong pipe. I think the heat is kind of awesome."

Dad's big hands tighten for a beat. Then he smiles. "It's fine," he says. "That's good to know." You know that saying, *I'm rubber and you're glue, and whatever you say bounces off me and sticks to you?* Well, Dad's rubber. Nothing bothers him. Everything bounces off.

He jots down some notes and then it's time for a slice of his world-famous quiche.

"You sure do eat good around here," Cal says. "I might have to stick around for a while."

Mom smiles, but it's forced. Nobody has said anything about how long Cal's staying, or why he's here in the first place. I just hope I don't have to babysit him anymore.

"They're shutting down the Res," Shelley says, and my appetite vanishes.

"Who is?" Dad asks.

"The parent association. They want to build a fence to keep kids from going there at night. They're setting up safety patrols, too."

An awkward silence settles over the table as this news sinks in. Oakwood, New Jersey, isn't the kind of place where bad things happen. It's a good town. A place where kids walk to and from school. At least that's what people said after Will's accident. Kids sneaking into the woods at night? A boy in a coma? That couldn't happen here. *But it had.*

"Well, that's a load of bull," Cal says.

Mom sighs. "Cal. Language, please."

Cal shakes his head. "They want to keep you kids so safe you never really live. A fence isn't going to stop anyone. It sure wouldn't have stopped me. Would it have stopped you, Max?"

That gross feeling washes over me. "I don't know."

"Reckless behavior gets people hurt," Mom says to Cal. "You of all people should know that."

Cal's smile vanishes. "That's not fair, Em. I took responsibility for my actions."

"You threw away every opportunity you ever had. You're living in your *van*, Cal."

"Are you serious?" Cal spreads his hands wide. "You think I *wanted* to lose everything that ever mattered to me?"

"You could have made different choices," Mom says more quietly.

"Well, I didn't."

A deadly silence falls over the table as Mom and Cal frown at each other. Shelley makes a *yeesh* face at me. Something bad happened with Cal, something Mom isn't telling us. Sometimes Mom doesn't like to talk about stuff like that, but we've been working on that with Dr. W. I don't know what to think about the town tearing down the roundhouse, but it's bothering me that Samantha said Will had water in his lungs. Will has a pool in his backyard. It was there when they moved in, and his mom almost had it filled in, but then Will grew up, and his pool was our pool in the summers. He's a really good swimmer. Better than me. It doesn't make any sense.

"Will had water in his lungs," I blurt out.

When I look up, my whole family is staring at me. This is the first time I've said Will's name since the accident.

Mom rests her hand on my arm. "Where did you hear that, honey?"

"Samantha Bovella."

"That doesn't sound good," Cal says. "Your neighbor found him, right?"

"The Dog Lady," Shelley says.

"Ms. Barrington," Mom corrects.

The dogs barking. My heart pounding.

I focus on breathing while my brain fights to show me something I can't quite see. The Dog Lady found Will on Brookside Drive, which is on the other side of the Res. No one knows how Will ended up all the way over there, just that she found him at daybreak, lying by the side of the road.

Unconscious. *With water in his lungs.*

"Is that the old lady with all the dogs?" Cal says. "How did she get involved?"

Mom squeezes my arm. "That's enough, Cal."

"I'm just trying to help."

She turns on him. "I didn't ask for your help."

Cal gives a sad little laugh and pushes back from the table. "On that note, I'm off to buy some wood." He looks at Mom. "You know, for that job I'm doing. For your *friends.*"

"In those shoes?" Mom asks.

Cal wiggles one of his yellow flip-flops like he's showing it off. "Yep."

Mom's gearing up for a lecture, but Shelley says, "I need

a ride to the library," and that makes Mom stop arguing long enough to check her watch.

"Shoot, it's past eleven." She looks at me. "How about you come with us to the hospital to see Will this afternoon? I can be back by two. Or you and Dad could meet me there."

"That works," Dad says. "I need to pick up some fresh clothes for them first."

Mom and Dad look at me, waiting for me to agree. But all of a sudden, I feel like I can't sit still another minute. I don't know how much of that is ADHD and how much of that is me freaking out. I should do the right thing and visit Will, but I don't think I can.

Cal opens the back door. Before he steps through, he looks back at me. "I could use some help," he says, and a weight lifts off my chest.

"Can I go with Cal?"

Mom and Dad share a glance. "Fine," Mom says. "Just be careful, Max."

Wood shopping is not what I expected. I guess I thought we'd go to a log cabin with a strange, bearded man who'd share a secret handshake with Cal and show us his special stash of fancy wood. Instead, it's driving to a salvage yard and watching Cal touch and sniff a bunch of beaten-up boards to find the perfect ones. They all look the same to me.

"For the record, I'm okay with you using me as an excuse to dodge your mom," Cal says as he examines a board that's covered in scratches but appears to have passed the sniff test.

"I didn't dodge Mom."

"Pshaw, give it a rest," he says. "I'm not her. We can be honest with each other."

I'm not sure I believe this.

"I love my sister, but she needs to loosen up," Cal says. "You know she used to make me redo my homework? My handwriting is garbage. She said I wasn't trying."

I think of the time Mom and I spent over the summer preparing for middle school, practicing the easiest ways for me to do writing assignments, according to the Manual of Max. We were just doing what my therapist wanted, to establish good work habits, but sometimes I wonder if I'll ever be good enough. It's hard growing up in a perfect family when you're not perfect. Even with my ADHD diagnosis, it still feels like Mom wants more from me.

"She checks my homework, too," I admit, and Cal sighs in sympathy.

"She just wants the best for you, man."

I know that, but it still sucks to feel like I'm not good enough how I am.

Cal starts whistling and I realize I'm drumming my fingers against a board. Instead of stopping, we make a weird little song together for a few minutes and crack up laughing.

"Let me spare you a little learning the hard way," Cal says. "There comes a point in life when you have to make a choice: Either you can be the guy everyone wants you to be, or you can be yourself. The difference is, that first guy's not real. *You're* real."

"Easy for you to say. You can drive away whenever you want."

Cal laughs and hands me another board to add to the pile on our rolling dolly thingy.

"Why'd you pick that one?" I ask.

"It's a feeling," he says. "I can tell when the wood is a good match for what I want to make. With reclaimed oak, you want to avoid the knots. This one has nice straight grain. No whorls. It'll be happy as a shelf. It won't want to bend or twist out of shape."

I run my hand over the surface of the board and a splinter snags my finger.

"Ow!" I shove my finger in my mouth and suck on it, which is gross, I know, but what else am I supposed to do?

"Be careful," Cal says with a laugh. "Sometimes the wood bites back."

8
NOT IT

MONDAY MAY BE A vacation day because of Rosh Hashanah, but Shelley and I still have chores, which means we're arguing about cleaning our bathroom. Mom and Dad have their own bathroom, and Shelley and I share the hall bath. Which means we share cleaning it, too.

"It should be illegal to share a bathroom with an eleven-year-old boy," Shelley says. Her arms are crossed. "There's no way I'm cleaning that toilet. *Not It.*"

"Then you have to do the bathtub."

"Nuh-uh. I did the tub last time. *Not It.*"

"You have to do one of them. Mom said so. You can't say *Not It* to everything."

Shelley scowls.

"Mom said what?" Dad calls from the office where he's working on his granola proposal.

"Mom said I need to be ready to meet the tutor at eleven, so there's no way I can clean our bathroom right now," Shelley shouts to him.

"That's not fair," I shout back.

Shelley laughs. "*Life* isn't fair."

"Just because you're a super nerd doesn't mean you get out of cleaning the bathroom."

She laughs again, and I wind up to flick her with the toilet brush, but then the front door slams and Mom's work heels click up the stairs. "Would you two stop bickering, please? I can hear you all the way outside. Our neighbors do not need to hear about how filthy your bathroom is. Test me on this, and you can clean the kitchen, too." She steps into the bathroom doorway and fixes an eye on Shelley.

"But the tutor—"

"It takes five minutes to clean a toilet," Mom says. "Get it done."

Shelley glares at me and I hand her the toilet brush, which makes her bite her fist and let out a muffled scream, and now I'm the one who's laughing.

It's a pain squeezing into the tiny bathroom together,

but I stand in the tub while I scrub it and Shelley holds her nose while she cleans the toilet. I circle the tub, but I can't remember where I started so I do it twice to be sure. We're almost at the part where Shelley and I argue about whose turn it is to vacuum the hair off the bathroom floor when the doorbell rings.

"I'll get it!" Shelley shouts, but Mom cuts her off in the hall.

"Don't even think about it," she says, and Shelley slinks back inside.

"Loser," I whisper.

"I hate you," she grumbles, but she doesn't mean it. At least not any more than I do.

"Max!" Mom calls. "Can you come down here, please? You too, Tim!"

"You have *got* to be kidding me!" Shelley says, and I race out of the bathroom before she can poke me in the side. I'm still laughing as I slide down the banister into the hall.

When I turn the corner into the living room, the laughter dies in my throat.

There's a young Black woman in the living room. She's wearing a long tan coat and a shiny badge on a beaded chain necklace. I recognize her from the hospital.

"Max, you remember Detective Sherman, right?" Mom says.

"Hi, Max." The detective smiles, but her voice is serious. "I have a few more questions for you. It shouldn't take long."

Mom sits on the couch and signals for me to sit beside her, so I do.

Detective Sherman takes the chair opposite us.

Dad walks into the living room a second later. When he sees Detective Sherman, his smile fades. "What's going on?" He takes a seat next to me, filling the couch the rest of the way. We're squished together like a can of sardines, but right now that feels good.

"Hello, Mr. Greenberg," Detective Sherman says. "The Schwartz family have asked us to check with Max again, in case he's remembered anything new."

Mom hasn't mentioned how Will was when they saw him at the hospital yesterday. I wonder if this is why. Do Will's parents think I'm lying? Do they think I hurt Will?

"It's okay, honey. They're just double-checking every-thing," Mom says, but she doesn't sound sure. Like she doesn't know if I'm telling the truth, either.

Detective Sherman opens her little flip pad. "During our initial interview, you stated that you came straight home from the roundhouse early on Monday morning. Did you stop anywhere else along the way?"

"No, I just ran home."

"Can you recall any other details? The time? Anyone you saw on the street?"

I look down at my fidget ring. All I can remember is being scared out of my mind.

"No."

Detective Sherman gives me a pity smile, and my stomach goes sour. Maybe if I didn't have ADHD, I'd be able to remember things like this better. I wish I could control my brain, but as much as some memories are seared into my mind, others disappear for me.

"Will had water in his lungs," I blurt out, and Detective Sherman goes still.

"Where did you hear that?" She smiles like everything's normal, but I can tell by the tone in her voice that my answer really matters here.

"Samantha Bovella."

"I see." Detective Sherman watches me for a few seconds. "Are you aware of any reason that Will might have gone to the pond next to Brookside Drive?"

A jolt of surprise runs through me. "We never go over

there. It's too far away and Will's mom said we shouldn't be by the road, there's too much traffic."

"Oh my god." Mom covers her mouth with her hand.

Dad wraps an arm around each of us. Dread pools in my gut. "Did he fall into the pond?"

The detective's face softens. "Will's clothing was damp when Ms. Barrington brought him to the hospital," she says. "We have not determined why at this time. Have you heard anything else, Max?"

I shake my head. There's nothing else I can tell her. If I knew what happened to Will, I would spill it in a heartbeat. "I never should have left him there."

"No," Detective Sherman says. "It was the right choice to leave, Max."

It's the same thing Mom said at the hospital, but I'm still not sure I believe it.

I woke up to Mom shaking my shoulder in the dark. At first, I thought I was dreaming. I didn't know where I was. Everything was backward and upside down.

"Max, wake up," Mom said.

I sat up and realized I was at home, lying on top of my comforter, with my head at the wrong end of the bed and my dirty clothes and sneakers still on.

Mom grabbed me and hugged me. "I didn't know you came home," she said. Her body heaved like she was trying not to cry. "I'm so glad you're okay."

"Mom, what's wrong?"

"It's Will," she said. "Will's in the hospital."

Somehow, I got up and we drove to the hospital. It was barely light out and everything was a blur until we stepped through the automatic doors to the emergency room, into bright lights, past busy people in blue and green scrubs, and down a long hall to a waiting room where we found Will's mom pacing, her eyes red from crying.

"What happened to him?" she asked me.

"I don't know—"

"They're keeping him sedated," she said. "They think he has a head injury. He can't even open his eyes." Her voice cracked. Mom tried to hug her, but Ms. Schwartz pushed her away. "No, Emily. I need to hear it from Max. How did Will get hurt? What happened to him?"

My stomach churned.

I thought of Jared screaming in my face, and cold, heavy

*shame snaked through me. I was twice Will's size. They expected
me to look out for him. I convinced Will to go to the roundhouse.
Then something terrible happened to him, and I wasn't even
there to help.*

"When did you come home, honey?" Mom asked.

"You went home?" Will's mom said. "Why?"

"We went to the roundhouse—"

"You went to the Res?" Mom said. "At night?"

Will's mom stared at me in horror. "What did you do?"

*"I'm trying to tell you!" I shouted. Tears pressed at my eyes.
"We went to the Res. Will didn't want to go, but we made him. I
got scared and ran home. I don't know what happened after that.
I'm sorry. I didn't mean for Will to get hurt...."*

Tears ran down my face as Will's mom broke into fresh sobs.

*"You shouldn't have gone out, but you were right to come
home," Mom said, wrapping her arm around me. "We'll figure
out what happened to Will, I promise."*

The kitchen door slams, and Cal's whistle fills the awful
silence in the living room. He strolls in from the hall and
stops dead in his tracks when he sees us.

"This is Detective Sherman," Mom says.

The detective smiles. "And who are you?" she asks.

Cal's face is pale beneath his stubble. "I'm, uh . . . I'm Cal."

"Full name, please?"

Mom gives Cal a funny look, and he says, "Calvin Nichols. I'm Emily's brother."

Detective Sherman jots this down. "Were you here on the night of September second?"

"No, ma'am. I live in Arizona."

She nods and shuts her flip pad. "Thank you for your time today, folks." She turns toward me. "Thank you, Max. I know it's not easy to talk about this, but any details you can remember could be a big help to us." She stands like she's ready to leave.

"Is that all?" Mom asks. "There must be something else we can do."

"We appreciate your cooperation," Detective Sherman says. "This is a difficult case. Unless some new information comes to light, we may never know what happened to Will."

Her words land like a punch to the gut. "You're giving up?"

Detective Sherman gives me the pity smile again.

"Hopefully when Will is brought out of sedation, he can give us some answers."

"What if he can't?" I'm trying not to think about what that might mean.

Dad squeezes my shoulder. "They're doing everything they can, Max. We have to be patient and trust the process."

"But it sounds like she's giving up!"

"I assure you, that is not the case," Detective Sherman says with a smile, but she doesn't sound very hopeful. She excuses herself, and Mom and Dad walk her to the door.

Cal comes to sit by me. "It's okay, bud," he says softly, but his voice is shaky, too.

I wonder if he's thinking what I'm thinking. That unless something changes, they are never going to figure this out. Something happened to Will out there. Something that left him unconscious by the side of the road, with damp clothes and water in his lungs.

Joey says he doesn't know anything. Jared and Luca said Will left after I did. Will can't speak for himself, and Detective Sherman has done everything she can.

Which just leaves me.

I'm *It*.

9

OHIO

DR. W HAS THIS technique for remembering to do something before you forget. It's called OHIO, which stands for "Only Handle It Once." The first letter of each word spells OHIO, like the state. It's a mnemonic device to help me do things right away before I get distracted.

When I lose my homework because I don't put it in my folder right away, she says, "OHIO." I have to keep the paper in my hand until it's in my folder. I can't set it down anywhere along the way. She knows I don't forget things on purpose. I just lose track of things. If I only handle something once, it's easier to get things done.

Just put the paper in the folder.

Just put the phone in my pocket.

Just do the thing.

That's why I'm sitting in Cal's van Monday afternoon, rattling my way to Bovella's, even though I really don't want to go back there. Samantha's going to fire a million questions at me. The thought makes me sweat, but it doesn't matter if I feel like barfing.

I have to find out what happened to Will.

This time, when we pull up to Bovella's, there aren't any cars in the parking lot. The sign is flipped to CLOSED and the lights are low behind the windows. Thankfully, I don't see Luca anywhere. Maybe he has the day off, seeing as they're closed for the holiday.

Cal pulls in parallel to the building, stopping the van right in front of the doors. "Just give me a sec to call the boss man so he can let us in," he says as he digs for his phone in the center console, which is piled with empty coffee cups and doughnut bags.

"It's okay. I think they know we're here."

Samantha Bovella is standing behind the glass front door. She turns a lock and pushes the door open, waving like she's been waiting on us forever.

"Looks like someone's happy to see us?" Cal glances at me, and my face heats up. Which makes zero sense. Samantha tore me up the last time we were here. We're not friends.

I climb out and get busy opening the back of the supervan.

"You need help?" Samantha calls over to us.

"Nah, we got it covered," Cal says at the same time that I say, "Sure."

Samantha props open the bakery door with a wedge and walks over. I hand her one of the reclaimed wood samples that Cal brought to show Mr. Bovella.

"I have to get back to the doughnuts in three minutes," she says.

"Doughnuts? I love doughnuts!" Cal practically shouts.

Samantha laughs.

"What?" he says. "National Doughnut Day is my favorite day of the year."

She shifts the board to her shoulder with a grunt. "I love doughnuts, too, but the commercialization of the calendar is so uncool. What's next, National Cotton Ball Day?"

Samantha walks away, and Cal laughs.

"She's all right," he says, and I think he's not totally wrong about that.

We unload the other wood samples and Cal digs around until he finds his drawings, laptop, and measuring tools. Once Mr. Bovella approves the plans for the display cases, Cal will start building them. He and Mr. Bovella sit at one of the little tables up front to go over everything while Samantha disappears into the back.

OHIO. Just go back there.

I follow her through the swinging door, where I find her dunking doughnuts in sugar. She looks up when I walk in, and my stomach drops.

I force myself to walk over to her. "I need to talk to you."

Her eyebrows rise. "About?"

"Will." My heart is thudding so hard I wonder if she can hear it.

She drops the doughnut she was sugaring. "Are you freal?"

I start spelling it out in my head.

"For. Real. *Freal.* Come on, Max, it's not that hard." She has her notebook out now.

"Detective Sherman came to our house this morning."

"She did? Is there new information?"

"No. They're out of leads. I have to do something."

Samantha studies me. "Why didn't you want to talk about it before?"

I don't want to tell her. Every molecule in my body is screaming at me to say something else. Anything else. But the only thing that will help is the truth.

OHIO. Just tell her.

"Will didn't want to go to the Res. We made him do it."

She gives me a cool stare. "And I'm supposed to believe you want to help him *now*?"

Heat flashes through me. "I messed up, but I'm trying to fix it."

She drums her fingers on her notebook. "What are you doing tomorrow?"

"Why?"

"We need to go back to the roundhouse. I'll skip work. My dad will get over it."

A wave of nausea hits. "I don't know if I can go back there."

She tips her head. "I thought you said you cared."

"I *do*."

"Then how else are we going to figure out what happened?"

"I don't know!"

She flings her hands in frustration.

I think about Will lying in the hospital. Ms. Schwartz pleading and crying. The paper cranes they made for Will at school. The meal trains and prayers at their synagogue.

Did I care? *Yes.*

Did I want to know what happened? *Yes.*

OHIO. I force myself to look Samantha in the eyes. "Okay. I'll do it."

10
OBSERVATIONS

TUESDAY MORNING, I WAKE up before everyone else, which never happens. It took so long to fall asleep that I feel like I never really slept at all. Every time I closed my eyes, I was in the woods again. Branches scratching my face. Leaves slipping under my feet. Heart pounding.

My head aches and my eyes are full of grit.

I sit up, groaning into the morning sunlight.

The house is quiet. The coffee maker hasn't clicked on downstairs yet, but a high-pitched mechanical whine is coming from outside. I lift my window shade. Cal's in the supervan doing something, so I grab a cold Pop-Tart, throw my sneakers on over my pajama pants, and go out.

The whine gets louder as I walk to the front curb.

It sounds like the time Dad ran over our garden hose

with the lawn mower. In two seconds, there was bright green plastic all over the lawn. This happened a few years ago, but Mom still warns Dad to put the hose up every single time he goes outside to mow.

The supervan's rear doors are open. As I walk around them, a board appears and slides toward me. It's moving fast and vibrating all over. Cal is on the other end, pushing the board through a machine, but when I try to grab the board to help, he hops out of the van and catches it himself. As soon as the board is finished going through the machine, the whining stops.

"Hey, bud," Cal half shouts. "Did I wake you?"

"No. I couldn't sleep."

"Me either." He props the board against the van door and grabs a pair of gloves and safety glasses off the counter. "Here, put these on for me, okay?"

I put them on. "What is that machine?" I shout over the whir of the motor.

"A planer," he yells back. "Watch."

He grabs another board from the stack on the van's floor, carries it to the other side of the machine, and feeds the end of the board into a narrow slot. As the board goes through the machine, the whine kicks up again. The end of the board that appears on my side is brighter, more yellow-white than grayish white, like the top surface of the wood has been peeled away.

This time, when I reach for the board, Cal gives me a thumbs-up. I catch the end of the wood and hold on, but it's vibrating so much my fingers go numb.

"Hold it level!" Cal shouts, and I lift my end of the board a little bit more, until it passes all the way through the machine and the whining stops.

Cal hops down to check it out. "That's what I'm talking about!" He runs a palm over the wood. "Smooth as a whistle. Yeah, buddy. Teamwork makes the dream work!"

I can't help laughing. For someone I don't know very well, Cal sure makes me laugh a lot. I kinda wish he had been around the last few years.

"Have you always liked wood?" I ask.

"Well, I wouldn't say I *like* wood—"

"I mean building things."

"Yeah." He props the board against the previous one. "I was always really into LEGO. But by your age, I liked building RC cars and modifying engines. That kind of stuff."

"Why'd you switch to wood?"

"There's this thing called money. . . ."

I pretend to turn and leave.

"Whoa, whoa, whoa," Cal says, laughing. "I'm just kidding. Stay, Max. Please."

I turn back.

He leans against the van's platform, his arms crossed. "Okay, seriously?"

"Seriously."

"Building with wood is like excavating a fossil," Cal says. "What the wood wants to be is already in there. You just have to get the other stuff out of the way. You have to find the heart that's hidden inside. If you do that, you can end up with something pretty special."

I imagine carving into a hunk of wood and accidentally breaking it. "What if you mess up?"

He shrugs. "You gotta make bad art to make good art. Now you gonna help me with the rest of these boards or what?"

We plane wood until my arms turn to noodles. We're nearing the end of the pile when my phone's alarm goes off. Today is the last day to do my writer's notebook assignment before school tomorrow.

OHIO. I take off.

"Where are you going?" Cal calls after me.

"Homework!" I shout back.

Inside, I check the launch pad and my book bag, but I

can't find my writer's notebook. I'm searching under my bed when I hear a noise from the office.

"Do you know where my writer's notebook is?" I ask, expecting to find Mom in there.

Instead, it's Dad.

He wipes his eyes and spins to face me. "Oh, hey, Max. I was just getting ready for my meeting tomorrow." His computer screen faces the door, and I can see a picture of the Twin Towers open on his desktop. I realize what day it is.

"It's 9-11," I say.

"Yes," he says. "Just thinking about some friends." He plasters a smile on his face and puts a hand on my shoulder. "School okay so far? No one's giving you a hard time, right?"

Dad knows all about being tall in sixth grade, because it happened to him, too. He also knows how to get over it. He's the rubber guy.

I wish I was, too.

"School's great," I say.

"Good," he says. "Now let's go find that notebook."

For our writer's notebook assignment, we're supposed to write about something interesting we've observed in the world. Like how people act or how something works. We can even make lists. They don't have to be sentences.

While Cal planes wood, I sit in the passenger seat to work. The sound of the planer is kind of nice. The white noise drowns out all the other channels so I can focus, like when I listen to music. I open my notebook and start listing observations . . . only it's more fun to draw them. I make a bunch of boxes and draw all the stuff in Cal's van. Gum wrappers. One lonely blue sock. A stack of round discs that play music in the van's ancient stereo system. I'm filling up pages so fast I might need another writer's notebook before the school year is out.

Observation: Cal's supervan is like a museum of his life.

I look in the busted glove box and draw the stack of manuals and parking tickets. A receipt for gas from Plano, Texas. Beneath that, a photograph of a blond woman next to a guy in flip-flops. Her arm is wrapped around him, but his face is cut out. It's got to be Cal, but I've never seen her before.

Someone raps on the passenger door, and I shove the photo back into the glove box.

It's not Cal peering in at me, though.

It's Samantha Bovella.

"You're good," she says, pointing at my drawings.

My face flushes hot. That's one of the other things about having ADHD: When I'm really interested in something, I go into this state called hyperfocus. I can work for hours and not even notice it. This happens when I play video games, and when I draw, but I can't do it on purpose. Hyperfocus just kind of happens to me.

I shut my notebook. "What are you doing here?"

"We're going to the roundhouse, remember? Luca gave me a ride."

I look through the supervan's windshield. Luca Bovella is walking up to Joey's house. His midnight blue Jetta is parked at the curb, just like it was the night we went over to Joey's.

A chill crawls over my skin.

"So?" Samantha says. "Are we going or what?"

The last thing I want is to go back to the roundhouse. I feel sick just thinking about it, but maybe the truth is hidden, like the shapes in the wood. There's only one way to find out.

"Yeah, we're going."

I climb out of the van and walk back to where Cal is lovingly sorting his freshly planed boards. "Hey, Cal? Can you do me a favor?"

"Sure, man. What's up?" He looks over at me and sees Samantha. "Oh, hello there."

She smiles. "Hi."

"I'm going to the Res with Samantha for a little while."

"Sam," she says. "Only my mother calls me Samantha."

Cal laughs and my face goes hot. "Anyway, I don't want Mom to freak out about us going there. We won't be long. Can you cover for me?"

"Sure." He nods. "I can do that."

I turn to leave with Samantha. *Sam.*

"Hey, Max?" Cal calls after me.

I look back.

He points at me with both hands. "Don't do anything I would do, okay?"

11
FINE, FINE

BY THE TIME SAM and I reach the end of my street, I want to turn back. There's a new red warning sign hanging from the chain over the entrance to the Res. WARNING! YOU ARE ENTERING THE SOUTH MOUNTAIN RESERVATION. NO ENTRY IS PERMITTED AFTER SUNDOWN. It's still early, but suddenly this seems like a very bad idea.

The Dog Lady's dogs are going nuts in her yard, jumping against her fence.

Sam hops over the chain.

It's now or never. I step over the chain like I'm stepping off the edge of the world.

Everything looks so different in the daylight. The leaves are starting to change, orange and yellow and red. Above the trees, the sky is pale blue with wispy white clouds. To anyone else this would look like something out of a story-book, but with every step I take it gets harder to breathe. My chest feels tight and my palms are sweaty.

Observation: The woods are scary quiet in the morning.

"I've never seen anyone hike in pajama pants," Sam says, making me jump.

I look down. I'm still wearing my plaid pajama bottoms and sneakers with no socks. I'm also carrying my writer's notebook and a sparkly blue pen, which was the first one I found in Cal's console. I don't have a water bottle or a bag, but at least my phone's in my pocket.

Meanwhile, Sam has a fleece over jeans, hiking boots, and a backpack with a water bottle and granola bars in the side netting. My stomach grumbles. I probably should've eaten more than a Pop-Tart before we left. "I have an extra water if you want one," she says.

"I'm fine." I didn't have any of that stuff the night we followed Jared and Luca into the woods. At least this time it's daylight out.

Sam hurries to keep up with me. Her short legs have to take two steps for every one of mine, but she's not complaining. "Is that your writer's notebook?" she asks.

"Yeah." There's a fresh rip along the spine and torn bits of paper hang out the bottom from when I've ripped pages out. I bet Sam's notebook still looks brand-new.

"Are you working on the observation assignment?" she asks. "I'm writing about contronyms. Did you know one word can have two completely opposite meanings? Like *clip*. *Clip* can mean 'to fasten' or 'to detach.' You can clip something *on*, but you can also clip it *off*."

I'm staring at her now.

"You know what else is a contronym?" she says. "Fine. It means excellent, or the best quality, but also just barely good enough. Good, or not good. Fine, *fine*."

We stare at each other.

Observation: Samantha Bovella can go a ridiculously long time without blinking.

"You really like words."

"I'm going to be a writer. Ms. Little says I have talent."

For a second, I'm let down that Ms. Little hasn't said anything like that to me, but also surprised that part of me wants her to. "What about the bakery?"

Sam's smile evaporates. "I don't want to work at the bakery. I'm going to be a journalist at a major national news outlet."

"I just thought, because of your family—"

"You must be a Taurus," she says with another frown.

"Creative, but a terrible listener. Why aren't you doing this with Joey? Aren't you guys besties?"

I can barely keep up with the changes in subject. "Not anymore. And I'm not a Taurus. My birthday is in October."

"Cool. Mine's in January. I'm a Capricorn."

We reach the top of the hill, and it takes me a minute to find the trail that Jared took. The leaves are a lot less trampled. I keep stopping to make sure we're going the right way, and to look for Will's glasses. He didn't have them when he got to the hospital, and the police didn't find them by the side of the road, either. Which makes me wonder where they went. Did Will lose them while he was running through the woods, trying to catch up to me? If so, why didn't I hear him crashing around? Why didn't he call out? I know why he didn't use his phone to call home for help—the service in the Res is terrible—but I would've heard him if he'd shouted.

The closer we get to the roundhouse, the more I sweat. It's hard work hauling my big body around, but this is different. This is nervous sweats.

A chipmunk darts past me and I half shout, which is ridiculous, but I'm on the edge of freaking out. Sam gives me a funny look and I tell myself to get it together.

A millennium later, I finally see a flash of red brick up ahead. My chest tightens.

"The police tape is still up," Sam says, as the round-house comes into view. The building looks different in the daylight. Smaller. More falling-down dangerous than haunted dangerous. The closer we get, the less impressive it is. Even the scary archway looks more like a busted old door than a gateway to the underworld. Which means I'm out of excuses. I didn't come all this way just to stare at the outside of the building.

OHIO.

I take a breath and duck through the twisted metal bands in the doorway. It's darker inside than I expected. I stumble down the slope of loose gravel and stop, waiting for my eyes to adjust as Sam scrambles down to join me. Something scurries away in the dark.

"Imagine being surrounded by vampires," I blurt out.

"What?"

"Nothing." I'm glad it's too dark for her to see me blush.

Yellow lines emerge from the shadowy interior.

More police tape.

The ground is uneven and covered in broken bricks, crushed beer cans, and twisted train tracks. In the center of the space, rusty railings circle a pit the size of my house. There's a broken bridge over the hole, with a big gap in the middle.

I can't figure out what it's for. "What is that thing?"

"They brought train cars here to fix them," Sam says. She points to a tall set of doors. "The trains came in and out over there. They turned them around on that bridge in the middle. It used to spin." She gets out her notebook and a flashlight. "Come on, let's work the grid."

She starts walking.

I follow, spinning my fidget ring while I watch the slow swing of her flashlight. We pass a million broken bottles, a busted grocery cart, and a faded plastic ride-on toy like the ones little kids use in their yards, but nothing that seems important to me.

"What exactly are we looking for?"

"Clues. Anything you recognize. Signs of a struggle." Sam sounds optimistic, but I can't imagine we'll find anything the police haven't already found. There are footprints everywhere, overlapping in the dust. I wonder which ones are Will's, and my stomach churns.

Sam flashes the light in my face. "Hey. Where'd you go? I was talking to you."

"I have ADHD," I blurt out.

I brace for her to joke or laugh, but she just nods. "Good to know," she says. "My cousin has it, too. Are you on meds? She says they really help."

"No, but I might try them. I just got diagnosed."

"Cool." She starts swinging her flashlight again.

We circle back to where we started.

Sam sighs. "Nothing. Let's check the pit."

I follow after her, but slowly. My legs drag like I'm walking through sludge.

"Did you guys climb over the bridge?" she asks.

"I didn't. I was only here for a few minutes." Hot shame washes over me. "I don't know if they did. Joey didn't say anything about it."

"Neither did Luca, but I know he's done it before. People dare one another to jump over the gap." She leans over the rusty metal railing. "Do you see anything down there?"

The last thing I want is to hang over the edge of the pit, but we came here to find answers. I grab the rusty railing and lean over it.

At first, I can't see much. The hole is too deep and dark. Sam's flashlight isn't strong enough to see everything clearly, but it catches on shiny objects below—more junk. And water. The bottom of the pit is full of dark, still water that sends a shiver up my spine. It could be ten inches deep or ten feet deep. There's no telling.

I imagine Will climbing over the pit, scared and

outnumbered, and wish we'd never come here. Or that I hadn't left him. Either way, I let him down that night.

Sam's flashlight catches on something. It's glass. The bottle is shaped like a cube, but rounded, with a long, thin neck. The label has a red diamond with a horseshoe at the top.

My heart stops.

I know that bottle.

I would know it anywhere.

It was halfway through the summer, and we were playing video games in Joey's basement like usual when Jared came down the stairs with a bottle in his hand. He saw us and made a face. "Do you brats always have to be down here?" he said.

Joey stood up. "We're not brats."

Jared snorted. "The evidence shows otherwise."

"Take it back," Joey said.

"As if." Jared hopped down the last two steps and started digging in the cabinet next to the wall, pulling things out and tossing them on the floor.

"Take. It. Back!" Joey shouted.

"Let's play again," Will said, but Joey wasn't listening. His hands were clenched around the controller.

When Jared stood up with the bottle and a stack of red cups in his hand, Joey threw the controller at him. Jared ducked, dropping the plastic cups and nearly dropping the bottle. "What the hell! What's wrong with you?" He scowled at Joey. "So you're a big man now? Is that it, little bro?"

Joey just stood there, his arms hanging at his sides.

"I tell you what," Jared said, shaking a plastic cup free. "Why don't you show me what a big man you are." He walked over and set the red cup on the table. Then he opened the bottle and poured. Brownish orange liquid swam past a red label with a diamond and a horseshoe.

Jared held out the cup. "Here you go. Drink up, big man."

Joey let out a breath and took the red plastic cup from his brother. Inside the cup was an inch of some kind of alcohol that stunk so bad I could smell it from the other end of the couch.

"What?" Jared said. "You scared or something?"

Will and I looked at each other, and it was like we were making a promise that no one else could hear: We won't do it. I looked at Joey with the same message in my eyes, but he didn't get it. He was too busy trying to show Jared how tough he was.

"Is there a problem, little bro?" Jared said. "Don't be a baby."

"I'm not a baby."

"Then try it."

Joey stuck his chin out and tipped the cup. He barely swallowed before he started coughing, spitting orange-brown liquid everywhere.

Jared burst out laughing.

Joey gagged, coughing even harder, like he couldn't breathe. Will grabbed his water bottle and gave it to Joey. Joey shoved the red cup at me, and for some reason, I took it. Or maybe he almost dropped it. Somehow, the cup ended up in my hands.

Jared looked at me. "Is it your turn next, big guy?"

My stomach dropped, landing somewhere near my shoes.

The game blared in the background while my mind raced. I didn't want to try it, but I did wonder what it tasted like, and I also knew Mom and Dad would be disappointed if I tried it, but maybe it would be fine, even though Will was looking at me like I was a total traitor.

Jared laughed and snatched the cup from my hand. "I'm just kidding." He laughed again. Then he shook his head and walked away, taking the cups and the bottle with the red horseshoe label with him.

12
PUZZLES

AT SCHOOL THE NEXT day, Ms. Little has a bunch of
words written on the board in a grid, like a crossword. Some
of them are vertical and some of them are horizontal, but
they all intersect. It looks kind of cool, but I don't know
how I'm going to focus on class today. All I can think about
is that bottle at the roundhouse. How it was just sitting there
in the pit. How it came from Joey's house.

We didn't bring it there—meaning me, or Joey, or
Will—but someone did, and that someone was probably
Jared. Jared, who made fun of us all the time. Jared, who led
us into the woods. Jared, who made Joey drink the alcohol
from their dad's bottle with the red horseshoe label.

I know what I think. Something else happened that

night. Something Joey hasn't told me. Something *no one* is talking about.

"We have to say something," Sam whispers.

My neck goes hot. "Not *here*."

Joey's hunched over in the bathtub, writing as fast as he can while Ms. Little circles the room checking our notebooks. If he hears us talking about this, I'm dead.

Sam leans closer. "The police need to know about this."

"Would you stop?" I whisper. "He could hear you."

Sam leans back, but she's not going to give up. When I pointed out the bottle at the roundhouse, she wanted to call the police, but I didn't know for sure that it was Jared's. He had a backpack with him, but I never saw what was in it.

What am I supposed to say to the police? That I think a bottle in the pit belongs to Joey's dad, but I have no idea how it got there or if it's really his?

Ms. Little circles past the couches and the beanbag chairs. The closer she gets, the faster I spin my fidget ring.

When I was drawing in the supervan, it felt good, but now I'm not so sure. We were supposed to *write* in our notebooks. All I have is a few pages of messy sketches. Part of me thinks I should hide my notebook and say I forgot it, but I don't *want* to hide my work. I'm just afraid to share it.

Last year, when I got my ADHD diagnosis, my fifth-grade English teacher had a hard time believing it. She didn't understand how a student as gifted as me could need accommodations. My therapist says people with ADHD can be brilliant and still have a hard time accessing their knowledge, but my teacher thought maybe I just needed to try harder. She kept saying I should slow down and use my planner during our parent-teacher conference, until I finally shouted, "I know what you want me to do! I just can't do it!"

That shut everyone up.

But what if Ms. Little says I just need to try harder, too? I can try as hard as I want, but I still operate according to a different manual.

Ms. Little walks up to Sam, who eagerly turns her pages, showing off a ridiculous amount of neat blue handwriting. Ms. Little murmurs something and Sam nods with a secret little smile. Then she folds down the corners on her pages and shuts her notebook.

I'm so busy watching Sam that I don't notice Ms. Little standing beside me until she says, "Max?" I jump halfway out of my skin, and she smiles. "Ready?"

Behind her, Joey laughs with Cam and Elijah. I try to ignore them and open my notebook. A century passes while Ms. Little looks at my pages. When she's done, I force myself to look at her eyes. Dr. W says it's okay not to make eye contact, but people like it because it makes them feel like I'm listening even though I can listen fine without it.

Ms. Little's face is very still. She's wearing tiny cat earrings today. I know I'm in trouble. I can practically see her adding me to the list of "disappointing" kids in her head.

Instead, she says, "You're very talented, Max."

My face goes hot. "My uncle's van is a mess."

She nods like I'm making perfect sense. "I would love to see you pair your illustrations with a written line about what you're thinking. Does that sound good to you?"

I hear the word "illustrations" and I'm back down the rabbit hole I fell into at breakfast, when I was trying to figure out the best way to use our tablet to draw. We don't have one of those fancy pens, but I think it's the best way to do it. I just have to figure out which pen—

"Max?" Ms. Little says.

Whoops, I was supposed to answer that.

"Yeah. I can do that."

After Ms. Little leaves, I lean over to Sam. "She's pretty cool." Sam nods, but she doesn't look at me.

Joey sees me talking to Sam and makes a kissy face. Great. I ignore him while Ms. Little reads *Wolf in the Snow*, which is a picture book without words. You might wonder how you read a book without words, but the answer is pretty simple: We look at the pictures and talk about them. Ms. Little says the key to learning is making connections. We ask questions to find answers. We're going to do the same thing in our writer's notebooks, using crossword notes for the books we're reading.

"Writing down the words that stand out can help identify the themes in a story," Ms. Little says. "The themes are the main ideas the author is talking about. Any ideas about what a theme might be for *Wolf in the Snow*?"

"Friendship," someone says.

Sam raises her hand. "Family."

"Adventure?" another voice calls out.

"Danger," Joey says, seeming to surprise himself.

Ms. Little writes these words on the board to form another crossword. "These are all great examples of themes. I'd like you to use this crossword exercise in your writer's notebook to explore themes in your independent reading this week, and let's see what you find."

I like this idea. It sounds easier than trying to write a paragraph. I can list a lot of words before I even have to decide which ones count the most. I can do that.

While Ms. Little talks, I start a crossword in my notebook. It has my name and Will's. Joey, Luca, and Jared. I add question marks around the names. I still don't know how Will got hurt, but something else happened that night. Something I am going to find out.

It's time to see Ms. Chen again. This time, she has a brown paper bag on her desk next to a partially eaten apple. The edges of the apple are turning brown, which grosses me out. It's also a little cold in her office. Her air conditioner doesn't whir on and off. It's just blasting.

"Hello, Max," Ms. Chen says. She flips to a new page on her yellow notepad. "How are you feeling today? Things going all right in your classes?"

"Things are good."

"How are you sleeping?"

"Okay." I rub my eye. It's itchy from not sleeping much last night.

She watches me closely, like I'm a puzzle she is determined to figure out. "Any trouble with friends?"

I shrug.

She waits.

"Are you going to keep asking me the same questions until you get an answer?"

"That's the general plan, but it's up to you to let me help you." She's right, but if I tell Ms. Chen what I'm thinking, which is that Joey's older brother took that bottle with the red horseshoe to the roundhouse, and that he obviously didn't tell anyone about it, Ms. Chen will go straight to Joey to ask him, and all Joey has to do is lie and I end up with both Joey and Jared officially mad at me.

It's not that I don't want to tell Ms. Chen what I'm thinking. I'd just rather not get my butt kicked.

"No, everything's good with my friends."

"Is there anything else you'd like to talk about?"

"Not really."

She sighs and clicks her pen shut. "Want to beat me at UNO again?"

13
THE SAME PAGE

THE HOUSE IS QUIET when I get home, which is weird, and the supervan is missing out front. It's the first time Cal must have gone somewhere without me, but I try not to take it personally.

Inside, I grab a couple of cheese sticks and check the calendar Mom keeps on the refrigerator door. Shelley's at debate club and Dad's at his meeting, but Mom should be home.

I find her upstairs in the office, which used to be our guest bedroom before Dad lost his old marketing job. Mom's still wearing her real estate clothes, but her pointy heels are off and she's standing behind her desk, staring at an old-fashioned photo album.

She looks up when she sees me. "Oh, Max. I didn't realize you were home."

"Where's Cal?"

"He had to run an errand."

"When will he be back?"

"I don't know, honey. We had an argument and he took off. It's what he does." She gives me a sad smile. "Did you two have fun working together yesterday?"

"Yeah. I learned all about whorls and knots."

I leave out the part about sneaking into the Res with Sam.

"Good. That's good." Mom glances at the album. The faded yellow pictures show two little kids playing in a sprinkler. "We loved this thing," Mom says. "Cal stayed in the water for hours, even if it was horrible for his eczema." She looks at me. "I'm glad you have this time with your uncle, but I need you to be careful. He doesn't always make the best decisions."

I don't know what to think of that. Cal may not seem like the most reliable guy, with his busted van windows and his stained T-shirts, but he really cares about this project for Bovella's. He took all that time picking out the wood and making it perfect. Something about Mom's comment feels familiar, but before I can put two and two together, she shuts the album.

"How was school today?" Mom asks. "Need any help with your homework?"

"No, I have this crossword thing, but it seems fun."

Her jaw drops. "Excuse me? Is this *my* Max describing school as fun?"

My face goes hot. "Well—"

"I'm just kidding, honey. I'm happy to hear it. All that work you did with Dr. Williamson is paying off. Is this assignment for the teacher with the bathtub?"

"Yeah. Ms. Little."

"Great. That's great." She sighs. "I feel like I'm not doing enough to support you. I'm just so stressed lately. I lost another client today."

She doesn't say why, but I wonder if it's my fault. "Because of Will's accident?"

"No." She walks over and squeezes my arms. "This has nothing to do with you. Your father and I have always found a way to make ends meet. We'll be fine."

I look at her wavering smile and wonder which version of fine we will be.

"Do you want to go to the hospital today?" she asks. "I have time before dinner."

I shake my head, and my stomach drops. Will's been in

the hospital for ten days, and I haven't been back to see him yet. I just can't go. Not until I have answers.

"Maybe tomorrow?" Mom says.

"Maybe."

But we both know tomorrow won't be any different. Not as long as I feel this way.

"It was a horrible accident," she says. "You're a good friend to Will."

I don't know about that, either.

"You can't make yourself responsible for other people's choices," Mom says. "Look at me and Cal. I gave up everything after your grandparents passed away, but there was only so much I could do for him. I was only nineteen. I was a kid raising a kid."

This time I'm the one who hugs her. We have this doorway in the kitchen where we mark our heights every year. When I passed Mom over the summer, she cried.

"You're so grown up, Max," she says. "I'm proud of you."

My stomach twists. I want to be proud of me, too.

Reading aloud isn't working for my homework today. After thirty minutes of rereading the same two paragraphs about

Earth's place in the universe and getting nowhere, I'm ready to throw my laptop out the window, so I go for a walk. Dr. W says it's super important to get exercise when I feel frustrated. Moving around gets the energy out of my muscles and changes the chemicals in my brain, which makes it easier to pay attention.

While I walk, I think about Will and the bottle we found. I think of how Jared scared me, and what might have happened after I left. What might *not* have happened, if I'd been there. Maybe Jared scared Will, too. Maybe he forced Will to do a dare. Maybe with that bottle.

On my way home, I look past our house to Joey's. Jared's car is in their driveway. The driver door opens, and Jared steps out. He doesn't say a word. He just stares at me.

My skin crawls.

Down the street, the Dog Lady's dogs start barking.

Then Jared opens the rear door, leans inside, and piles his arms with brown paper grocery bags. The last thing I expected to see is Jared getting groceries.

He glances over at me again, and I make a beeline for our house. When I get back to my room, I'm out of breath. My writer's notebook is open on my desk. I'm supposed to make a crossword of the themes in this cool graphic novel

Ms. Little gave me called *Fly on the Wall*. I already read twenty pages in class, which is a record for me, but I don't feel like writing. Instead, I draw Jared. His car. The groceries. I don't know what to make of it. Then I'm drawing other things. Me and Will and Joey at the entrance to the Res. The branches on the trail. The roundhouse, the water, the graffiti on the bricks. Then the bottle. I don't like thinking about any of it, so I pretend I'm filing the memories away, and that once they're in my notebook, they can't touch me.

I have to pee, but I don't want to stop. It feels so good to let all of this out. I draw and draw. All I can think is, what happened? *What happened to you, Will?*

"Max?"

I look up. The room is much darker than it was before I started drawing. I'm exhausted. And starving. And I have to pee so bad I'm afraid I'll wet my pants.

Mom's in the doorway. "Dinner's ready."

Cal doesn't come inside for dinner. He doesn't come in for breakfast Thursday morning, either. On my way to school, I take a glass of orange juice and a couple of toaster waffles

to the supervan, where I find Cal sprawled across the driver's seat in yesterday's clothes.

I knock on the window and he shoots up. "What's
wrong? You okay, Jenny?"

I freeze.

Cal wipes greasy hair out of his eyes and blinks. "Oh.
Hey, Max."

I want to ask who this Jenny person is, if she's the girl in
the cut-up photo I found, but Cal's so wrinkled and pathetic
that I just hand him the juice and the waffles, which he
inhales in a few big bites, followed by one long slurp of juice.
"Thanks, buddy. You're a lifesaver."

"No problem."

Cal sighs. "Sometimes I wonder what I was thinking,
coming here. Your mom's a super smart lady and I owe her a
lot, but we've never really been on the same page."

"Why did you come here?"

He blinks. "I guess you could say I didn't have anywhere else to be."

"Did you sell your house or something?"

"No." He looks away. "I never had a house. Had a
pretty okay apartment, but I couldn't keep it. Besides, I've
got everything I need right here." He pats the steering

wheel. "I like traveling light. It's easier that way. Less to lose, you know?"

In that moment, he looks anything but light.

Overhead, the sunlight fades. Thunder rumbles as a spatter of rain hits the windshield. Cal leans forward, his head in his hands. "I've gotta get out of here," he says.

And I don't think he just means getting out of the super-van, or even our house.

I get to school, and Sam has this look on her face like she just licked a lemon. For a second, I wonder if she's mad at me. Then I smile at her, and she smiles back.

I squeeze under the four-person table she's sitting at and lean close enough to whisper. "We should go to Brookside Drive next."

"Okay," she says, but she doesn't sound excited, which is weird.

"I just thought you might want to go, because we went to the roundhouse together."

"No, I want to."

I take one of her emoji erasers, because I can't find mine

and she always has extras. "I don't get how Will ended up over there. It's the opposite direction of home."

"It's sweird, yeah," Samantha says.

"Can you come over Saturday?"

"Sure. I have to work, but I'll make up an excuse." She's still acting strange, and I get this weird feeling she's mad at me, but maybe I'm just imagining it. The truth is, I don't know her very well, but it's nice to have someone to do this with. Way better than doing it alone.

"Teamwork makes the dream work," I say, and she rolls her eyes, but there's a little smile in the corner of her lips.

I'm still thinking about how nice it is to have a teammate when I get home and find Cal vacuuming the supervan, which shows just how desperate he is to avoid Mom. I have no idea how to get them on the same page, but I do have an idea of somewhere we can go.

Somewhere that might help.

Cal looks up, and I shout, "Want to go to an arcade?"

14
GAMES

WHEN WE WALK INTO Yestercades, Cal's face lights up, and not just from the neon signs and flashing screens. "I wish I had a place like this as a kid," he says. "I would've *lived* here."

"You didn't have arcades in Arizona?"

"No, there were arcades, but money was tight. Grandpa's disability paid the bills, but it sure didn't pay for video games. Grandma had to quit teaching to take care of him. They relied on your mom a lot. When they passed away, there was nothing left. Nothing but bills. Healthcare in this country is a total crock, you know?" He shakes his head.

I nod like I knew that, but Mom never talks about this stuff. Her parents died in a car crash when she was in college. Cal was a kid, so Mom dropped out to take care of him, which I only know because Mom likes to remind Shelley that she's lucky all she needs to do is study.

We get our wristbands and start gaming. Cal is great at the old video games, like Dad, but he's even better at pinball. I've never really played pinball much, but Cal shows me the secret moves on the *Ghostbusters* pinball machine and I'm hooked. If you hit the right combination of paddles and ramps, mini games appear on the display screen. While I play, the noise of the arcade makes everything else disappear. I'm gone, lost inside the game. I've just summoned the Hell Hound for a really cool mini game when someone shoves my back, hard.

My hips slam into the pinball machine. "Oof!"

Strong hands grip my shoulders and spin me around. It's Jared. Luca Bovella and Joey are behind him. Cal is nowhere in sight. He said something about beating the record on *PAC-MAN*.

"What did you say to the police?" Jared says, jabbing my shoulder.

"What?"

"You know what I'm talking about." He grabs my arms, hard. "You think this is all a game, huh?" He has Joey's same blond hair and blue eyes, but the whites of Jared's eyes are shot through with red, like he hasn't slept in days. He shakes me, and I hunch down. "Tell me what you said," he grits out, his face close enough for me to smell his breath.

"Nothing!" I look at Joey, but he's tucked up against the side of the *Galaga* machine like a shadow. I'm starting to wonder if I *did* do something.

"Stop lying," Jared says.

"I'm not lying! I don't know what you're talking about, I swear."

"I told you this was a bad idea," Luca Bovella says. "He doesn't know anything."

Jared tightens his grip. "He was the only other one there. It had to be him."

Luca makes a face like he's tasting something sour but says nothing.

"You can't just rat us out like that," Jared says. "The police came to our *house*. They questioned my *dad*. You're the only one who could have known about that bottle."

Understanding rushes through me. The police know about the bottle.

Sam.

She must have called them.

I look at Luca, and he shakes his head, just slightly.

No. Like he's telling me not to do it. I don't know why, but instead of ratting Sam out, I stand up a little taller.

"I don't know what you're talking about."

"Yes, you do," Jared says, tightening his grip.

"No, I don't!" I'm trying not to cry as tears fill my eyes. I don't know what Jared did with that bottle the night Will got hurt, but there's one thing I understand perfectly: Jared's willing to hurt me to hide it. And I have no idea how to make him stop.

"You may be my size, but I can still crush you," he says.

I look at Joey for help, but he's staring at the floor. My bones feel like they're cracking beneath Jared's fingers. I'm about to scream when Cal comes around the corner.

"Whoa, whoa, whoa!" Cal shouts, wedging himself between me and Jared so Jared has to let go. "That's enough, fella. Back it up." Cal puts his hands up while Jared stares us down.

"We're not done talking," Jared growls.

"You are for now," Cal says. "Why don't you boys move along."

Jared shifts his glare to Cal.

"We don't want any trouble," Cal says, his hands still up. "Just go. Please."

Jared thinks about it, his face red with rage, but Luca claps a hand on his shoulder. "It's not worth it, man. We don't want to mess with this guy. Dude needs a shower."

Jared laughs and flicks his hand at Joey. "Come on, bro. Let's bounce."

Joey trails after them like a pale little ghost, but before he disappears around the corner, he looks back. I wait for something—an apology, a threat—but he just frowns and walks away.

"What was that about?" Cal asks as he starts the supervan for the drive home. We tried playing more games, but all the fun had gone out of Yestercades. After a sad round of air hockey, Cal said we were better off getting out of there. It was almost dinnertime, anyway.

"Seriously, what was up with those kids?" Cal asks again. He leans back in the supervan's captain's chair, making it clear he's not moving until I answer.

"They think I called the police on them."

"Whoa. What now?"

I shrug. I'm never going to that arcade again.

"No way, Max. You can't say something like that and

expect me to let it go. You gotta level with me, kid. Is there something going on that I should know about?"

He's right. Someone should know about the bottle we found, but apparently the police already do, and that's what matters. What did Jared do that he's so determined to cover up? Maybe Jared is the reason Will got hurt. Maybe *Jared* hurt Will.

"*Max.*"

"Those are the kids who went into the woods with us that night. With me and Will."

"I see. And?"

"They think I'm trying to pin the accident on them."

"Are you?"

I turn to look at him. "Are you kidding me?"

"Okay, okay. Relax, kid. I had to ask. Does this have anything to do with your disappearing act the other day?"

"Maybe."

"How's the girl play into it? She wasn't there that night, was she?"

"No, she's just my friend." I reconsider. "Or at least I thought she was."

"Seems like she's got a pretty sharp head on her shoulders."

"Yeah." Sam is the smartest person I know, but she called the police. She sent Jared after me when I asked her not to. I may be the same height as Jared, but I'm no match for him. Especially when Luca and Joey just stand there and let Jared push me around. *Again*.

I groan and flop my head against the headrest. "I hate this place."

"Look, kid. If everyone likes you, you're doing life wrong," Cal says. "There are always going to be people who don't like you. Forget those people. You don't need them."

"Easy for you to say. Some of us actually like having friends."

He laughs. "I'm just saying, those boys aren't on your team, Max. I hope you know that."

I don't want Cal to be right, but he might be. Part of me thought Joey and I would figure this out and go back to being best friends again, but things can never go back.

Everything's changed. We've changed.

"Yeah, I know."

"It sucks, but it's the truth, man. Some people are not friend material. If anything like that happens again, just walk away. It's not worth it, trust me."

I manage a small smile.

"Feeling better?" he asks.

"Yeah."

"Glad I could help." Cal drums his fingers on the steering wheel, clearly pleased with himself, and a feeling like being caught picking my nose washes over me.

"Why did you really come here?" I ask.

His fingers go still. "It was a good time for a visit," he says, glancing over at me, "but I'm not gonna lie to you, kid. I thought maybe you could use some help, with your friend being in the hospital and all. Your mom, too. It seemed like a lot to deal with, you know?"

My face goes hot. Of course he came here because of what happened with Will. It's not like he just showed up to build some cabinets. Or to hang out with me.

"Look, your Mom and I fight a lot, but we talk when it matters," Cal says. His words slowly sink in. He and Mom have been talking. About *me*.

Somehow, this makes me feel like the biggest loser.

"Listen, I know a little something about life," Cal says. "There are some real sucky parts, but things get better. Your friend's gonna pull through this. I believe it with my whole heart."

My throat clenches. I manage a nod.

"Don't let those jerks dull your shine. Okay?"

I nod again, but I'm not sure it's that easy.

If I want to find out what happened to Will, I have to keep pushing. And Jared is not going to like it.

15
ANGER MANAGEMENT

I'M EXPECTING SAM TO hide from me on Friday morning, but instead she corners me outside of Ms. Little's classroom. Her olive skin is flushed, and her eyes are determined. She braces her arm on the cinder-block wall to keep me from going into the classroom.

"It was the right thing to do," she says. "I had to call the police. There's a code of ethics about this kind of thing. Journalists have an obligation to report the truth."

She looks so sure of herself, but right now all I can think about are the bruises on my arms. "That's nice, but your brother seems to think that I'm the one who ratted them out."

Her brow furrows. "No, he doesn't. Luca knows I called the police. Jared took that bottle to the roundhouse. Luca had nothing to do with it, he promised me."

"Right." I don't know who she's kidding, but Luca is not on Team Max.

"The police needed to know about the bottle. It's an important piece of evidence."

"I know."

"Then why are you mad at me?"

"Because! Jared came after me at the arcade! Luca was there. He let it happen."

"He did?" She takes a step back, and I take some deep breaths. I'm so angry I want to storm out of the building, and I never skip school. I hear Joey's voice coming from inside Ms. Little's room and my chest tightens. I know I should just accept that he's not on my team anymore, but I can't. It hurts too much.

I start to charge into the classroom to yell at Joey, but Sam catches me by the arm. "I'm sorry," she says. "I didn't know Luca did that. I'll talk to him about it." She sounds sorry, too. All the spark has gone out of her voice.

The bell rings. It's time to go into class.

"Do you still want to go to Brookside Drive tomorrow?" Sam asks.

Do I?

Sam went behind my back to the police. Her brother let

Jared threaten me. But I never would have made it to the roundhouse without her. I never would have found that bottle.

"Yeah. I do."

The plants in Dr. W's office need watering. At least that's what she says after the first five minutes of our session pass in silence. I'm not trying *not* to talk, I just can't seem to get past the anger that is bubbling up inside me. For how sad and afraid I've been this last week, now I feel like I'm going to say something awful. Or cuss. Neither is okay.

Dr. W hands me a jug, and we go about watering her plants. I'm careful with the cacti, which only need a drop. I take care of the plants hanging over the window, too, because they're easy for me to reach. Then I turn around and trip over my own big feet, spilling water everywhere.

"What the hell!" I shout. The words just fly out, like my mouth is possessed.

Dr. Williamson raises her eyebrows.

"Sorry. I shouldn't have said that."

"No, this is good. You're angry. Let it out. Who are you angry with, Max?"

"No one. I'm fine."

"Max." She takes the watering can out of my hand. "Sit, please."

I flop into the big squishy chair in the corner. She sits on the couch and props her cane against the arm. "Tell me one good thing from this week."

I blow out a long breath. "My English teacher liked my drawings."

"Good. Now one bad thing."

Jared's face looms in my mind.

Dr. W takes a gummy bear from the bowl on the coffee table. "It's okay to feel angry, Max. I know you regret some of your choices, but making mistakes is part of being human. We all fail to live up to our own standards or do things we feel are wrong. It's also possible to be in the wrong place at the wrong time. It's important to recognize what was your responsibility, but also what wasn't. That might result in feeling angry. You have to let those feelings out."

The pressure building in my chest says she's right, but I'm afraid of what will happen when I let go. Of who I might hurt.

"Sometimes you have to let a feeling go over and over

again in order to accept what happened and forgive your-self," Dr. W says. "Now tell me, who are you angry with, Max?"

"Jared," I blurt out.

"Why?"

"He thinks because he's older than us he can do what-ever he wants!"

"Good. Who else?"

"Joey. He's being such a jerk!"

"Who else?"

Sam. Luca. My mom. Cal. The entire town. Even Will.

"And what about you, Max?" Dr. W asks softly. "Are you angry with yourself?"

I nod. For some reason, I'm crying.

"It's okay, Max." Dr. W says. "Let it out. It's easy to hide from pain, but we really only start to deal with it when we let ourselves feel it."

"I don't want to feel like this."

"I know," she says softly. "All we can do is work through the emotions as they come. You have to forgive yourself, Max. Don't let shame control you. Let it go. If you kick your feelings under the rug, you'll just keep tripping over them." She smiles.

I bark out a laugh.

"While you're here, you can be as angry as you want. It's easy to lash out when you're processing complex emotions. Pain breeds pain. Hurt causes hurt. If we let the steam out here, you're less likely to explode at home and feel badly about it."

"I need anger management now. Great."

She smiles. "This is *trauma* management. Anger is only one of the emotions you'll feel."

We talk for the rest of our hour. Dr. W ends our session with a high five. "You did good work here today, Max."

For once, I feel like I did.

16
BROOKSIDE DRIVE

BROOKSIDE DRIVE IS ON the other side of the Res, past the roundhouse, as far away as you can get from our street. That's where the Dog Lady found Will. Everyone thinks he got lost trying to follow me. That he went in the wrong direction. Will's smart, though. He would have known to turn around and keep an eye on each tree as you pass it to make sure you're going in a straight line. I mean, he grew up playing in the Res, too. He knew those woods. But if he lost his glasses . . . If Will couldn't see, he may not have known where he was going. He might have gotten that lost.

Cold, alone, and shouting my name.

The idea makes me so impatient to get back on the trail that I stand up in the middle of helping Dad and

Shelley with our 3D printer on Saturday morning and start to leave.

"Where are you going?" Shelley asks as she tries to feed the filament into the printer. She has it lined up right, but the filament falls out. The spool is catching higher up.

I reach over her and straighten the feeder.

Shelley pokes me in the side. "What is it?"

"The line is caught."

"You could just tell me so I can do it myself. This project is important."

"Imagine not having a life," I snap.

Shelley rolls her eyes. "What are you even saying?"

Dad clears his throat. "How about we give your brother a little space to operate, seeing as he's the only one who knows how to run this thing."

Shelley grumbles but moves out of the way so I can untangle the filament. I get the feeder working, but the spool is running low. "We need more filament."

Dad blows out a breath and smiles, but it's forced. "Sorry. We've been trying to cut back on expenses while I'm still out of work."

"Don't worry about it," Shelley says. "I'm sure we have

enough left on this spool." She glares at me like I'm being a jerk.

"*What?*" How was I supposed to know we were cutting back?

Shelley shakes her head like I am the world's densest substance and sprays the printing tray with glass cleaner so the 3D print will release easily.

My phone buzzes in my pocket. Sam's outside.

"I'm going on a bike ride," I tell Dad, with a tiny twinge of guilt.

"Okay," Dad says, cheerful as ever. "Don't forget your phone."

Outside, Sam's leaning against the supervan chatting with Cal. I jog over to them. We need to get this done while Mom's still at her open house. "Hey. You ready?"

"Morning to you, too," Cal says with a grin.

Sam tips her head. "Your funcle was just telling me a story about how you used to take off your dirty diapers and throw them over the side of the crib."

Flames erupt on my face. "I didn't—I don't—"

Sam grins. "Just kidding."

"What did you just call me?" Cal asks her.

"Funcle. Fun uncle."

"I like it," Cal says. "You're all right with me, Sam. You kids be safe now."

"We'll be back soon," I say, pulling Sam along.

She double-times to keep up. "You're in a rush."

"I don't have a lot of time before my mom gets home."

"Okay." She's quiet as we hop over the chain and head into the woods. After a while, she taps my arm. "I talked to Luca," she says. "He's sorry about the arcade. Jared was just mad about the police coming to their house, and Luca didn't want him to be mad at me."

I bet he's sorry. *Sorry he got caught.* "Did Luca let Jared think I called the police?"

"I'm sorry. He shouldn't have done that."

"What a jerk," I say, and Sam goes quiet. I feel that anger bubbling up inside me again. I kick rocks along the trail as we go. By the time we get to the top of the ridge, I'm panting. Sam stops to take a swig of water. This time, I accept the bottle she offers me.

We both gulp our waters, then turn in the opposite direction of the roundhouse and keep going. "Keep an eye out for Will's glasses," I say. "They haven't found them yet."

"Vinteresting," Sam says, and I can't help laughing. "You like that one, huh?"

I shake my head, but she's smiling, too.

After a while, a flash of paved road appears ahead. Off to the left, water. I steer toward the pond. It's not big enough to be a lake, but plenty big enough for a small boat. There are NO FISHING signs posted all around, and more police tape. My heart speeds up the closer we get.

We reach the water, but instead of footprints or drag marks, there's nothing. Just loops of yellow police tape by the road, and mud and leaves and pond scum along the edge of the water. My sneakers sink into the mud with every step, so it doesn't make any sense.

"Where are Will's footprints?"

Sam gets her phone and taps at the screen.

"What are you doing?"

"Looking up how to track someone, duh." She frowns. "Nothing's loading."

"Yeah, the signal is bad up here."

"Well, that explains a lot." She stuffs the phone back in her pocket. "It rained a few days ago. Maybe everything got washed away."

"Maybe."

We both take pictures, me from up high and Sam from

down low. After we circle back and forth around the edge of the pond, we climb the incline to the road. There are tire tracks along the shoulder. Footprints, too, but few leading back the way we came.

Did Will just accidentally run in the wrong direction? Or did Jared scare him, too? And if Will fell into the pond, how did he end up by the road?

It doesn't make any sense.

I turn to face the woods. The leaves are all colors now. The breeze picks up, making the branches wave. One summer, during my Roblox phase, me and Will and Joey built a village out of sticks in Joey's backyard. We dug a mine and stacked stones for houses. Every day, the village grew, until it was a whole world. We had weapons and sheep pens and trees made of leaves. Then it rained one night, and everything washed away. We built it back. Over and over, so many times. Until one time, we didn't. And now you can't tell that village was ever there.

Sam taps my shoulder. "There isn't much here. The police must have done a thorough sweep." We walk around a little longer, taking more pictures and bending down to examine every little piece of trash, but there's no sign of Will's glasses, or of Will's footprints.

I kick a rock into the road. "This was a waste of time."

"No, it wasn't," Sam says. She's busy scribbling in her spiral-bound notebook. "All we can do is observe. Who knows what will prove useful? Clues are usually pretty obvious when you look back at them, but hard to see when they're right in front of you."

My phone alarm goes off. "I need to get back. My mom will be home soon."

"Me too," Sam says. "I may have skipped my shift today."

We take one last look around the pond and follow our own trail back across the Res. The sun's almost overhead, so it's got to be lunchtime by now. This is taking way too long. I'm just hoping Mom isn't waiting to question me about where I've been or what I've been doing.

I'm so busy hurrying down the slope to the end of our street that I don't even notice how much the Dog Lady's dogs are barking at first. Then I look up and see the angle of her roof cutting into the sky, and the memory hits me like a wave lifting me clear off the ground.

After I left the roundhouse that night, it was so dark out, I couldn't see where I was going. All I knew was that I had to get home. Immediately. Right that second.

My arms pedaled as I ran downhill, but the leaves were too slippery. I kept losing my balance. Tripping. Falling over my big feet and smacking into branches.

My face stung. My lungs ached.

When I saw the house lights again, I burst into tears. I couldn't help it. It was just too much. The roundhouse. Jared scaring me like that. Why did he have to be so mean?

I hated Jared.

I hated Joey.

I hated myself.

I got to the end of our street and grabbed the wooden post that the chain hangs from like it was a lifeline while I tried to catch my breath. Maybe I was crying too loud or maybe I was shouting cuss words, but either way the Dog Lady's dogs started barking. She kept some of the dogs inside, but there were doghouses behind her fence, too.

"Shut up!" I shouted, but they just barked louder.

Jumping against the fence, making it shake.

I should go home. I should go back. I should be tougher. My parents were going to be so mad. It didn't feel right to leave my friends back there, but what was I supposed to do? Go back and fight Jared and Luca? I didn't even know how to fight. That wasn't the type of thing Mom and Dad encouraged. We weren't the kind of people who got into fights. We knew better.

But then who stops those kinds of people?

I needed to calm down, but my brain was so full of thoughts, it sounded like TV static.

I let out a groan that was more like a shout and turned back to the Res. My friends were out there, but I was so tired. All I wanted was my bed.

I wiped my eyes and turned for home. As I looked up at the Dog Lady's house, a light clicked on.

One upstairs.

Then one downstairs.

A shadow appeared in the window, making my heart stop.

I jumped the chain and ran for home, with her dogs barking every step of the way.

"Max! Are you okay?" Sam's hand is on my arm. I'm frozen at the end of the sidewalk. I blink, remembering where I am . . . and that I just realized something huge. "She was home."

"What?" Sam says.

"Sam, she was home! The Dog Lady. I remembered something else. When I was coming home that night, her lights came on. She was *home*."

Sam sucks in a breath. "In her interview in the paper, she said she was at the emergency vet all night. One of her dogs ate something bad and she had to take it to get help. That's why she was on Brookside Drive. That's how she found Will."

Only she wasn't.

We stare at each other, the full meaning hitting both of us. *The Dog Lady lied.*

"Samantha Valentina Bovella!" a man's voice booms.

I turn to see Sam's father standing on the sidewalk with my mother, and Cal.

Sam sighs.

We are so busted.

17
DRY FIT

MOM HATES LYING. SHE was always pretty patient when I forgot stuff, but if I lied? It was like the apocalypse. It took a lot of talking with Dr. W for Mom to understand that lying is an impulse for me. Sometimes I forget something. Sometimes I'm confused. Sometimes a lie just pops out, because I'm worried I'll get in trouble if I tell the truth. Especially if I messed up. Mom's supposed to try not to take it personally, and I'm supposed to be honest when we talk it out.

"Why did you tell Dad you were going for a bike ride if you were really going to the Res?" Mom asks.

"I thought he'd say no if I told him the truth."

We're rehashing yesterday's choices at Sunday brunch, which is something Mom likes to do after we've had a chance to cool down. She sent me straight to my room yesterday. Sam's father just glared at me and told Sam to get in the car.

"I understand," Mom says, "but what if you got hurt?"

"He's okay, Em," Cal says.

"You're not helping," Mom tells him. "We need to know where Max is for his safety."

Cal puts his hands up. "You're the boss." But when she looks back at me, he winks.

"You're grounded for today," Mom tells me. "And you owe your father an apology."

"I'm sorry I lied, Dad. Can I still go outside to help Cal today?"

Mom opens her mouth, but Dad beats her to it. "You can go as far as the curb, but that's it." Mom doesn't look entirely thrilled with this amendment, but she nods.

Shelley makes a face at me, and Dad says, "Watch it, or you're grounded, too."

"I'm too old to be grounded."

"No one's too old to be grounded," Mom says.

Dad laughs. "Wait until you hear how much butter I used this week."

Mom swats at him with the back of her hand and we get back to trying Dad's revised savory granola flavors. His first meeting didn't go well, but he says he's not worried.

He has one more group he's taking his proposal to, and he thinks they'll be a great fit.

I wish I could bounce back like that, but Sam and I are stuck. Both of us are grounded, and neither of us knows what to make of the Dog Lady's lie. Why would she say she was at the emergency vet when she was really at home? How did she end up on Brookside Drive? I don't know, but it's all I can think about while I help Cal outside.

Today we're dry-fitting the pieces for the display cases. It's bright and sunny out, even if it is a little chilly. It's September 16. Two weeks since Will's accident.

They're supposed to wake him up this week. That's what Mom said before she left to take his parents a casserole.

But what if Will doesn't wake up? What then?

"Hey, Leonardo da Vinci," Cal says. "Penny for your thoughts?"

I'm surprised to find Cal next to me, looking at my writer's notebook. I've been drawing the display cases as we put them together, along with a sentence about each step, like Ms. Little suggested. I've even added some notes about the wood and the design.

"These aren't half bad," Cal says. He leans against the supervan and flips through my drawings. My heart skips when he gets to the drawings of the Res, but either he doesn't know what he's looking at or he's playing it cool.

"They're okay, I guess."

"Okay? Dude. Give yourself a little credit." He smacks the page with the back of his knuckles. "You're putting something into the world here. That takes guts!"

I don't feel brave. I feel like it takes me way too long to write a few words.

"Are these part of a collection?" he asks, studying the drawing of the roundhouse more closely. "You into creepy places or something?"

"It's the roundhouse."

He raises a brow. "That's where you went the night your friend got hurt?"

"Yeah." My throat feels tight saying this stuff out loud. "Don't tell Mom about these."

His hand goes over his heart. "Dude. I would never."

He shuts the notebook and passes it back to me before he turns back to the display cases. The parts are organized and labeled with all of the joints rough cut into the wood. We're slotting the pieces together, but we aren't using any glue or nails so it will come apart again. That way Cal can make sure each piece fits perfectly before he applies the glue. A dry fit is like a rough draft for furniture, which makes sense when you think about it.

Cal picks up two pieces from the pile and taps them together with a rubber mallet while I hold the ends steady. Piece by piece, the first case comes together, until we get to the very top piece, which is beautiful thick oak board that will double as a counter. It's supposed to slot into the side pieces with these cool triangular teeth called dovetails that lock the wood into place.

Only the dovetails don't fit.

My stomach lurches in horror.

Cal shrugs. "Not the end of the world."

"But you'll have to make it again."

"Better than finding out later, when I can't change it."

He's right, but I can't believe he can just wave off a big mistake like that. My skin is buzzing just from seeing those pieces of wood fail to click together. I look down the street, toward the Dog Lady's house, and another wave of panic hits my stomach. Sam and I have to do something, but I'm not sure what. Either I go to the police with this new memory, or we ask the Dog Lady ourselves. I don't like the idea of turning her in because what if I'm wrong? What if there's something else I'm not remembering? Mom would be mad at me for accusing a neighbor of something . . . and what am I even accusing her of in the first place?

There's no easy solution here.

Just like with Cal's display case.

"I broke my first phone this summer," I blurt out. "It was on my bed and I didn't see it, and I just, like, sat on it. And my butt cracked the screen. I didn't know butts could do that."

"Tough luck," Cal says. He messes my hair. "You're gonna be okay, kid. You're only a beginner at messing up. Talk to me when you're in the major leagues."

He's got the same goofy grin on his face as always, but I can't help wondering what he did that was so bad that Mom's mad at him all the time. What kept him from visiting?

"Why is Mom always on your case? Did you do something wrong?"

He blinks. "I killed a guy."

A beat passes.

He laughs. "Nah, I'm just kidding. I messed up a little. Or maybe a lot. I overreacted to a situation and someone got hurt. By me. But the guy lived, I swear. And I made a promise to myself that I would never use violence again."

I say the words in my head. That sounds a lot like something I would say.

"Why did you do it?"

Cal stares up at the sky for a moment. Blows out a breath. "He hurt someone I love."

I remember the cut-up photo in the glove box, and Cal calling out the name *Jenny*.

"Is that the girl in the picture?"

Cal flinches like he's been slapped. "You been going through my stuff, kid?"

"Not on purpose. I was just drawing things for my notebook." I flip to the pages with the items from Cal's glove box. "I saw a picture with a blond lady in it. I'm sorry."

He nods slowly. "That's my girlfriend. Or was." He lifts the top off the display case a little too fast and the side panel crashes down. "Whoops. Grab that for me, will you, kid?"

Cal disappears inside the supervan.

Within seconds the buzz of the band saw fills the air.

Which means we're done talking, for now.

18
STANDOFF

THERE'S A BUZZ IN Ms. Little's room as we get out our writer's notebooks. I'm excited to have her check mine, too. I mean, it would be better if Joey wasn't giving me a sad face emoji every time I glance in his direction. I keep waiting for him to say something about what happened in the arcade, but so far he hasn't. I don't know what Jared and Luca are hiding, but I'm not going to get anything out of Joey. I'm going to keep trying, though. We may not be the kind of people who get into fights, but that doesn't mean I can't fight back.

I lean over to Sam. "We should talk to the Dog Lady next."

"Yeah," she says. "I can say it's for the school paper."

"She won't go for that. She lets her dogs chase the reporters off her lawn."

"Maybe she's just shy?"

I shake my head. "She barely gave any interviews. She hates people in general."

Sam frowns. "I'm good at this, Max. Trust me, I can get her to talk."

"Okay. Are you still grounded?"

"According to my dad, I'm grounded for the rest of my life," she says, "but sometimes you have to take risks in the service of truth. I don't care if he doesn't like you."

The words hit with a sting. "He doesn't like me?"

"He thinks you're, like, a bad influence. He asked me if you shave yet."

My entire face goes hot. "I don't."

Sam's mouth falls open. "I'm sorry, I shouldn't have said that. He was just mad that I skipped my work shift, but it was worth it." She smiles, but I can't shake the gross feeling in my stomach. Mr. Bovella thinks I'm a bad guy. He thinks I'm like Jared: big and trouble. The kind of kid who hurts other kids. All because I'm so much bigger than Sam. But what about Luca? He just stood there and let Jared come after me at the arcade. How am I the bad influence here?

I sink into my chair, my knees bouncing as Ms. Little reads today's picture book: *They All Saw a Cat*. In it, many different animals see the same cat, but the images are all totally different. What they see depends on their perspective. Their eyeballs. Their height.

Like the way Mr. Bovella sees me.

I glance at Joey while Ms. Little reads. He's biting his nails. They look raw.

A jolt of guilt stabs my heart, but there's nothing I can say right now to fix things between us. Even if I apologize for getting them in trouble, Joey won't tell me what happened that night. He's as scared of Jared as I am. Just like how the cat looks huge and terrifying to the ants, as long as Joey sees his brother that way, we're stuck. And I don't see how that will change.

It's weird sneaking past my own house, but if Mom knew I was going to accuse one of my neighbors of lying about Will's accident, she'd lose it. Apparently that idea doesn't bother Sam at all because she's whistling as we make our way up the opposite side of the street.

"Will you keep it down?"

She tips her head. "Where's your sense of adventure?"

"It got grounded."

Sam laughs, and I have this weird moment where I feel like I'm back in time, when it was me and Joey and Will walking along this sidewalk, laughing and skipping cracks and competing to see who could hold their breath the longest or eat the most acorns (spoiler: do NOT eat acorns unless you want to spend an entire afternoon on the toilet). Only now it's me and Sam, which is both nice and awful at the same time, because I miss my friends. I miss Will. And Joey.

We reach the end of the street and cross over to the Dog Lady's house. The chain-link fence is latched but not locked. There's a walkway leading to the front porch, which has a small wooden dog gate on it, but there are no dogs in sight. *OHIO.*

I unlatch the gate as quietly as possible. "Run!" I whisper to Sam, and we take off.

We make it through the gate onto the porch a split second before two giant mutts come running up the steps behind us, jumping like they want to eat us for dinner. I'm not even scared of dogs and my heart is pounding. I feel like I'm floating but in a bad way.

"Get out your notebook or something," Sam says. "And try to look less tall."

I get my writer's notebook and dig in my bag for a pen, but I can't find one.

Sam hands me a pencil.

My face burns. "Thanks."

"There's so much to remember in life," she says. "It's unreasonable." Before I can even answer, she rings the Dog Lady's doorbell. "What's her name again?" Sam says.

My brain goes utterly blank. "Ms. . . . B-something. Oh my god, I can't remember."

Sam lifts the lid to the Dog Lady's mailbox and looks at a piece of mail. "Barrington. Got it." As she puts the mail back, the door cracks open and I do my best to hunch down.

"Can I help you?" the Dog Lady says, her face barely visible behind the door.

"Hello and good afternoon, Ms. Barrington," Sam says. "We're students from the local middle school and we could really use your help with a project. We need to interview a local—"

"No interviews." The door starts to close.

"Please!" Sam implores. "We'll fail our class if we don't get this interview."

The door stops moving.

"It will only take five minutes, I promise," Sam says. She looks up at me.

"We'd really appreciate it," I manage, though my voice cracks.

After a long pause, the door swings open enough to reveal the Dog Lady. She's a lot shorter than me and is holding a small black dachshund to her chest like a shield.

"You have five minutes."

Sam smiles. "Thank you so much, Ms. Barrington. First, I'd like to say how much I admire you. What you did for Will Schwartz was incredible. You saved his life."

The Dog Lady barely nods.

"The night that Will got hurt, one of your dogs was sick?"

"That's right."

"Which one?"

The Dog Lady blinks.

"Sorry, I'm just such a dog lover," Sam says. "We have two at home."

"Did you know that dogs have fifteen thousand hairs per square inch of skin?" I blurt out.

The Dog Lady frowns.

Sam gives me a look. "Yes, dogs are amazing creatures," she continues. "Anyway, which one of your fur babies was the culprit that night?"

"Finn," the Dog Lady says. "My black Lab. He must have gotten into something during the day. What class did you say this interview is for, again?"

Sam smiles. "It's for English Language Arts. We're interviewing people we admire, and we both really admire what you did that night. What's it like to be a hero?"

I expect the Dog Lady to blush, but instead her lips flatten. "I never asked to be a hero."

"Well, we are who we are, right? So, you left at what time for the vet?"

"Around one a.m."

"And you went to the emergency vet—"

"In Garfield." She readjusts the dog in her arms. "Are we done here?"

"Almost. That all makes sense except for one little problem. . . . Max here saw your lights come on later that night. If you were at the emergency vet, who turned them on?"

Ms. Barrington's lips part in shock. Her small dark eyes fix on me, making me want to crawl under the porch and hide. "You're one of those boys."

"What boys?" Sam says, but the Dog Lady is already shaking her head.

"How dare you scare my babies like that in the middle of the night." The dachshund in her arms growls. He doesn't seem scared at all.

"I didn't do anything to your dogs."

"You call what you did nothing?" She scoffs. "Children

these days are entirely devoid of morals. You should be ashamed of yourself. I have nothing more to say to you."

She steps back and slams the door in our faces.

"That went well," Sam says, and I groan. "No, I mean it. We got a few things out of her. She says she left at one a.m., but you guys went out around two a.m., right?"

"I don't know. I didn't have my phone with me."

"No worries," Sam says. "The police report said two a.m., and if you guys were gone for, say, an hour, that means you saw her lights come on around three a.m. She claims she was at the vet until early morning, when she found Will. That does not add up, any way you slice it."

"Yeah, I know. She's lying."

Sam nods thoughtfully. "The question is, why?"

"Maybe she doesn't want anyone to know she was home?"

"Because?"

I search my mind but come up empty.

"S'okay," Sam says. "We just need to keep digging."

Sam heads back to school to get a ride home from Luca, who thinks she stayed late to work in the library, and I walk into our kitchen to find Mom sitting at the kitchen table with red cheeks and tissues in her hands. Dad's next to her, with Cal and Shelley.

It's so quiet I assume I'm in trouble again. "Mom, I can explain—"

"It's Will," she says, her voice breaking into a sob.

Shelley starts crying and Cal puts an arm around her.

My heart is in my throat. "What happened?"

Dad looks at me. "They lifted Will's sedation at the hospital today."

"He didn't wake up," Mom says. "I'm so sorry, honey. Will didn't wake up."

19
SYSTEMS FAILURE

MOM NEVER LETS ME skip school, but this time she makes an exception. As we walk into the hospital Tuesday morning, the silence wraps around us like a tomb. I try to focus on my breathing like Dr. W said, but it's not helping much. My heart feels like it might explode.

The door to the ICU whooshes open.

The hall is wide and lined with machines and people in scrubs. It smells like bleach. Our shoes squeak against the linoleum with every step. I try to land my sneakers so they make as little sound as possible, but I feel like everyone's staring at me. Mom says hello to different nurses as we pass by. The closer we get to the end of the hall, the more my chest tightens. By the time Mom stops in front of one of the closed doors, I'm ready to run back the way we came.

But I can't. I have to do this. For Will.

"Maybe you can talk to him about school," Mom says. "If it's too much for you, just tell me. We don't have to stay long." She pushes the door open, and I feel like I'm falling.

The room is dark, and quiet. A machine beeps somewhere, but softly. The blinds are closed. Will's dad is asleep in a chair in the corner. Get well cards and paper cranes fill the windowsill behind him. Flowers. Balloons. Even a few plush toys.

We step past a flimsy curtain and Will is there, in a bed so big it makes him look tiny.

His mom is sitting in a chair next to the bed. She's holding Will's hand.

His mouth hangs open a little, like he's deep in sleep.

When the Dog Lady found Will, he was unconscious. The doctors said he had signs of a head injury. The medically induced coma was supposed to end when the doctors stopped the medicine, but Will's brain is still asleep, and no one knows when it's going to wake up again.

"Max," Ms. Schwartz says, and I tense up, but she smiles. "I'm so glad to see you again. I want to apologize for how I spoke to you the last time you were here. I was terribly upset that day. It will be good for Will to hear your voice."

She gets up and offers me her chair.

I sit down. The seat is warm, like she was sitting there for hours.

"Let's get some coffee, Gina," Mom says. "You'll be okay for a few minutes, Max?"

I don't feel okay at all, but I nod, and Mom steers Ms. Schwartz out of the room. I set the *Minecraft* Steve bobblehead that I brought for Will on the table next to his bed. Will's dad is snoring softly with his arms crossed over his chest and his head propped against the wall. There are dark circles under his eyes, but he's just sleeping. If I clapped my hands, he'd wake up.

Will wouldn't. It doesn't seem real. Or possible.

We did this project on the human body in fifth grade. We had to pick one of the five major body systems and make a model of that system on a T-shirt. I picked the skeletal system and made the bones out of modeling clay. Joey picked the digestive system because, well, poop. Will did the nervous system, with a pretty amazing brain he made out of mini marshmallows.

As I sit there looking down at Will, I wonder if his body systems know they are in a coma. Are they on pause? Are they just whirring along, waiting for him to sit up and walk out of the hospital? Does Will know he's asleep, and if he does, can he hear me?

"Hey, Will." I feel silly for talking out loud, but Mom said that hearing familiar voices can help him. He might be able to hear us. His mom has been reading his favorite books, trying to catch his brain's attention so it will snap out of this slumber and wake up again.

I lean closer, so Will can hear me better. "I remembered something, Will. The Dog Lady's dogs were barking that night, and her lights came on."

I back up to check his face. Nothing.

"She's lying about not being home, but I don't know why."

Will breathes, his face still.

"Jared's hiding something, too. What did he do after I left? Can you hear me?"

I put my hand on Will's arm. It feels small and bony beneath his cowboy pajamas. All I can see is him running through the woods, lost, without his glasses. Scared, and alone. If I hadn't convinced him to go to the roundhouse, he would probably be okay right now.

"I'm sorry," I say, and my voice catches. Tears rush into my eyes. I swallow hard, breathing them back. "I'm sorry it took me so long to come here, and I'm sorry we made you go to the roundhouse. I'm going to find out what happened. I promise."

Will's chest hitches, and for a second, his eyelashes twitch.

I hold my breath.

The door cracks open behind me, and a woman in pale blue scrubs walks around the curtain. "Hello, there. I'm Angelica. I'm here to adjust Will."

At the sound of her voice, Will's dad stirs in his chair. His eyes pop open.

"Good morning, Mr. Schwartz," the nurse says.

Will's dad returns her hello and looks at me in surprise. "Hey, Max. I didn't realize you were here. Can I get you to scoot that chair back from the bed for a minute? We need to change Will's position to keep him comfortable."

I stand and move the chair, while Mr. Schwartz and Angelica pull back the blankets and shift Will's body. The nurse pulls up Will's pajama top to adjust a plastic disk stuck to his chest, revealing big brown and yellow splotches all over Will's rib cage.

"How did he get those bruises?" I ask.

Will's dad glances at me. "The doctors say the bruising is from cardiopulmonary resuscitation. CPR."

There was water in his lungs.

"The doctors gave him CPR?"

"No. Will was breathing when he got here."

Someone else gave Will these bruises. Someone who was there that night. Someone who knew CPR. *Like a lifeguard.*

A chill runs over my skin.

There's only one lifeguard who was there that night.

Will's dad tucks the blankets around Will's body. I should tell him about the Dog Lady's lie, but I don't know what to say. I know she's lying, but I don't know why, just like I don't know what Jared and Luca and Joey are hiding, and what that has to do with Will.

Mom and Ms. Schwartz come back into the room with coffee for Will's dad. They talk quietly and share hugs. Mom looks at me and raises her eyebrows.

I nod. I'm ready to go.

We say our goodbyes and I give Will an awkward hug. His mom looks so sad I want to scream. It's not right that everyone's telling lies while Will's in here like this.

When we get to the car, Mom lets out a long, slow breath.

"What do we do now?" I ask.

She turns to look at me. "The doctors are doing what they can. They say his brain activity is improving and the swelling has reduced significantly. That's all good news."

"But he's not waking up."

"Not yet." She squeezes my hand. "But I believe he will."

20
CHEAP SHOT

I NOTICE A FEW kids looking at me as I walk into school on Wednesday. Maybe they've heard that Will didn't wake up. I keep my eyes on the floor and slam my locker shut. Ms. Little smiles as I walk into English, but I don't feel like smiling. My brain keeps going back to those bruises on Will's chest. If they were from CPR, Luca must have had something to do with it. I hate fighting with friends. I'd rather respawn into enemy territory, but I know what I have to do.

Sam perks up when she sees me. "Max! Why didn't you text me back? I looked at Ms. Barrington's interviews, and she told the reporter it was her *German shepherd* that got sick, not her black Lab. Why are you looking at me like that? Is something wrong?"

OHIO.

"Luca knows CPR, right?"

"What?"

"Will is covered in bruises. His dad said someone did CPR before Will got to the hospital, and we both know it wasn't the Dog Lady."

Sam's mouth falls open. "You think Luca hurt Will?"

"I think Luca knows CPR, and Jared brought that bottle there for a reason. Something bad happened, and Luca's helping him cover it up."

"Why would you say that?"

"Because it makes sense."

She shakes her head. "Luca wouldn't lie to me like that."

"He's a lifeguard, Sam."

"He's not like that!"

"Neither am I! If I hadn't made Will go out that night, none of this would've happened, but I did make him go, and something bad happened, and someone gave Will CPR. I know you don't want it to be your brother, but I thought you wanted to find out the truth."

Sam's face is full of panic. "Luca said he left after you and Will."

"Maybe he's lying. You think someone else came along and gave CPR to Will? That doesn't make any sense. It had to be Luca."

There's this long pause while Sam stares at her hands. Then her whole body slumps in defeat. "Oh my god," she says. "Oh my *god.*"

Ms. Little starts talking, so I spin my fidget ring and do my best to listen. Sam sniffles every once in a while. Halfway through the period, she asks to be excused to the nurse's office.

I watch her hurry out, her brown ponytail swinging.

Everything I said is true, but I still feel bad. Sam doesn't want her brother to be guilty, but something terrible happened that night, and Will's in the hospital because of it. Sam has to get that. I keep waiting for her to walk back through the door, but she never comes back.

When class finally ends, I head to my locker to send Sam a text. We have to keep our phones in there during the day. If you get caught with one in class, it gets taken away.

I spin the numbers on my locker and dig through the books piled in the bottom, but I can't find my phone. It's not in the wire mesh bin stuck to my locker door, either. I pat my pockets but they're empty. Did I leave my phone at home again? I try to remember if I grabbed it from the launch pad that morning as I set my book bag on the locker shelf and rip the zipper open. I better not have lost it. Mom will freak out. I'm already down one phone this year. I dig through my bag as fast as I can. My fingers finally hit plastic in the front zipper pocket, where I usually keep my lunch. I yank out my phone and unlock the screen as fast as I can. I'm almost out of time between classes. The bell is going to ring any second.

I'm sorry, I write Sam.

I know she understands what's going on here. Maybe she just needs a minute to get over it. It hurts when you find out someone isn't the person you thought they were. You never see that coming. I know. That's how I felt when Joey turned on me.

I'm about to ask if she went home early when someone barrels into my side and my phone goes flying. The open locker door whacks my face, making me yelp. I press a hand to my cheek and turn around just in time to see Joey swing his backpack at me. It feels like a bag of rocks when it hits me in the guts and folds me in half.

"What the hell?" I shout, as Joey winds up again.

His eyes are squeezed shut.

"Joey, stop!"

He doesn't say a thing, but there are kids gathering

all around us. Joey's bag crashes into my arm, making my elbow scream. I can't believe he's doing this, attacking me in the middle of the hall, but Joey was always the one who took cheap shots when we were gaming. Will never did that, not once. But Joey? He'd do anything to win, and he just expected us to get over it, because it was just a game. Well, this isn't a game. I'm so sick of Joey not being on my team.

Before I know it, I'm grabbing his book bag and holding on to it while he tries to tug it free. "What is wrong with you?" I shout. "Why are you doing this?"

"You have to stop," Joey says. A tear slides down his cheek.

"Stop what?"

All around us, kids are shouting and egging us on.

"That's enough!" an adult voice booms.

The space around us opens up like a vacuum releasing air.

A teacher I don't know says, "Let go." I realize he's talking to me. He assumes I'm the big kid, beating up on the little guy.

I drop Joey's book bag and step back.

The teachers are doing their best to clear the hall, but all I see are faces laughing. Jeering.

Enjoying the show.

21
CHOICES

PRINCIPAL FLEMING IS A fan of restorative circles. We sat in them to talk about Will on the first day of school. They're supposed to build bonds between us. I have to admit, it was kind of nice to sit together and be honest with one another. It felt a lot better than being stared at.

There's no way I'm sitting in a circle with Joey, though. Two people can't make a circle, anyway. I can barely stand to sit next to him in the front office waiting for our parents. We're not supposed to talk to each other, but as soon as the secretary gets on the phone, I turn to Joey.

"What's wrong with you?"

He flinches at the sound of my voice, which just makes me angrier.

"We're going to get suspended for this," I say.

He sighs. "I know."

"Then why did you do it?"

"I didn't have a choice," he whispers.

The secretary hangs up her phone call, so I sit there seething. Waiting. A parent walks in to pick up their kid for a dentist's appointment, and I try again.

"What do you mean, you didn't have a choice?"

"You don't get it." Joey picks at the lint on his T-shirt. He doesn't look like he'd want to fight a lint brush, much less his onetime best friend.

"Come on, J. It's *me*."

Joey looks at me, and I try my best to smile at him, even though it's hard.

For a split second, his face opens up. "Jared said I had to warn you," he whispers.

"Why?"

"He's going to kill me."

"Because you're talking to me?'

"Because you won't stop."

"What do you mean, *stop*? What did I do?"

Joey looks at the door to the office and blanches. His father is signing in. I only have seconds left to find out why

Jared sent Joey after me. Other than generally hating me, there has to be a good reason, because Joey's dad is definitely going to kick Joey's butt for this.

"Why did Jared want you to fight me?"

Joey doesn't say a word. Just acts like I don't exist.

"Joey. You have to tell me. For *Will*."

He looks at me. "Jared saw you talking to the Dog Lady. You have to stop prying."

Joey's dad comes in, and Joey's face closes up like a mask. Mr. Peterson is a big man, but more than that, he's got this heavy energy around him, like a black hole. When Joey's dad tells him to get up, Joey does it as fast as possible, with his head hanging low.

They go in to talk with Principal Fleming while I sit there wondering why Jared would care if I talked to the Dog Lady, or why he would force Joey to attack me over it. It must have something to do with whatever Jared's hiding, but I can't figure out what that might be.

A few minutes later, Mom shows up. She's in sweatpants with unbrushed hair. "*Max*." She hugs me, and I almost start crying. Which is ridiculous. I'm not the one in a coma.

"Dad's on his way," she says into my ear. She takes the seat next to me, hand on my arm.

"Did Will wake up yet?"

"No," Mom says. "Not yet."

A few minutes later, Dad rushes through the door in his office clothes. "Hey." He gives Mom a quick hug before he takes the seat on my other side. "I had to wrap up my meeting."

I feel terrible. "Sorry, Dad."

"No, it's no problem," he says. "We were finished, anyway."

Joey and his dad emerge from Principal Fleming's office.

"Frank," Mom greets him as Dad says, "Hello."

"Emily. Tim." Mr. Peterson says their names like they taste bad.

As he walks out the door, Mom turns to Dad. "I know," Dad says. "I'll call him later."

Then they're gone, and it's our turn.

Principal Fleming's office is covered in framed pictures, diplomas, and awards. There's hardly any space left on the wall behind her desk. She temples her fingers and looks at me. "Max, I understand you've been under a great deal of pressure lately, with what happened to Will Schwartz. I empathize with your situation, however that is no excuse for fighting."

"He's very sorry," Mom says.

"I wasn't fighting," I blurt out. "He attacked me."

Principal Fleming smiles grimly. "We seem to have conflicting stories about the nature of your incident. It can sometimes be difficult for our more mature students to understand how even a small action can be harmful to others."

"Our more *mature* students?" Mom says. "He's *eleven*."

"Just because he's tall for his age doesn't make him more responsible for this," Dad says, as I hunch lower in my chair, my face burning.

Principal Fleming clears her throat. "Rest assured, we will fully investigate, including a review of our camera footage. For now, I have to send Max home for his own benefit."

Mom's mouth drops open. "You're suspending him?"

Dad puts a hand on her knee and squeezes.

"In the event of a first physical altercation such as this, up to a two-day suspension is dictated by the School Board Code. If our investigation finds grounds for bullying or any other extenuating circumstances, we will review the referral for suspension."

"Surely there's some flexibility in the rules considering our son's account?" Dad says.

"I didn't hit him back," I say.

"This is our procedure," Principal Fleming says. She pushes a piece of paper across the desk. "I'll give you a few minutes to write down your account of the events on this incident form. Please know we are committed to ensuring the safety and well-being of all children in our school. We will not tolerate bullying in any form."

I can't tell if she's promising me or threatening me.

Dad shakes his head in frustration.

"It's okay, honey," Mom says.

For the first time in my life, I'm suspended. And it doesn't feel good at all.

I'm expecting Mom to drive us home, but as we leave the middle school parking lot, she turns our minivan in the opposite direction of Dad's car, toward the highway.

"Where are we going?"

"Dr. Williamson has an opening this afternoon."

Actually, that doesn't sound so bad.

For a while Mom drives in silence. At the next red light, she slaps the steering wheel and says, "I can't believe that principal! She took one look at you and decided she knew exactly what happened. All because you've got Dad's height!"

"Yeah."

Mom sighs and glances over at me. "Sometimes I have to remind myself that you're only eleven. I'm so sorry, Max."

"It's okay."

"No, it's not, but it will be. We'll make sure they know you didn't do anything to Joey. Next time, just walk away. Don't take the bait."

"I didn't hit him. I just grabbed his book bag so he'd stop."

"Yes, but you could have just walked away," Mom says. "Sometimes that's the best choice." She sighs again. "This is my fault. I never should have let you spend so much time with your uncle. This is just like Cal. Exactly the kind of thing he would have pulled."

"I didn't *pull* anything. Joey jumped me in the hall. And Uncle Cal didn't tell me to pick a fight. He said I should walk away, too."

Her brow furrows. "He did?"

"Yup."

She watches the road for a few seconds. "Well, clearly this whole situation with Will is causing a rift between you and Joey, so maybe you should stay away from him for now."

"I've been trying to."

"Well, try harder. I don't know what else to tell you."

I don't know what else to tell her, either. I still can't figure out why Jared sent Joey after me for talking to the Dog Lady. All I know is, he did. And I couldn't stop it.

That's what I tell Dr. W.

"You aren't helpless, Max," Dr. W says. "You didn't ask for this fight to happen, but you can make a different choice next time."

"The principal thinks I'm a bully."

Dr. W leans in. "It doesn't matter what someone else thinks you are, Max. They can call you whatever they want, but that doesn't make it true. Even the one-thousandth time they say it, it still won't be true. You get to define yourself."

I think of Ms. Little's letter from the first day of school. She said the same thing, but it doesn't feel any truer now than it did then.

"You are bright, resilient, and creative," Dr. W says. "You're also a human being who sometimes makes mistakes, but we all do, in our own ways. Now let's talk it out."

So that is what we do.

22
VENEER

CAL SAYS IT'S TIME to pick out a finish for the display cases. He still has some modifications to do, but he wants Mr. Bovella to choose the finish color now. This means a trip to the bakery. Seeing as I'm home on suspension, Mom says it's okay for me to go with Cal.

"Just don't get into any more trouble," she says, but she probably doesn't want me moping around the house all day. There's been no change with Will. I asked her first thing this morning, but Will still hasn't woken up.

On the way to the bakery, I see a rolled-up newspaper lying in a driveway and think of Sam. She hasn't returned any of my texts, which is no surprise. I accused her brother of lying. Of course she doesn't want to talk to me. It's almost lunchtime, so I'm relieved she'll be in school instead of at the bakery. Maybe I can explain everything to her when I get back on Monday after my suspension is over.

Cal laughs.

I realize he's been talking, and I missed it. "What?"

He glances at me. " 'What,' like what does that word mean, or did you miss all of that?"

My cheeks grow warm.

Cal is quick to squeeze my shoulder. "Hey, it's okay, buddy. I space out all the time. I can repeat my awful joke about varnish." He winks. "Did you hear about the wood-worker who died when he fell into a vat of varnish?" He pauses for dramatic effect, hands off the steering wheel. "It was a terrible end, but a beautiful finish. Da-dun-dah!"

I half laugh. "That's a terrible joke."

"Imagine being terrible at jokes," Cal says, and I laugh for real. "Am I doing that right?" he asks, and I laugh even harder. It's not the same as playing with my friends, but I appreciate it.

"What are you so busy thinking about over there?" he asks.

"Sam's mad at me."

"What for?"

"I think her brother's hiding something about what happened to Will."

Cal lets out a low whistle. "That's heavy, man. Is this something we need to share with your parents? Your mom was pretty upset about that fight at school. Your dad, too."

Shelley also warned me not to do anything that would end up on my permanent record, as if I'm going to be competing for scholarships like her.

"I don't know yet," I tell Cal. "But when I do, I'll spill."

"Good," he says. "I don't recommend learning the hard way. It sucks."

It does suck. I got into a fight just like Cal, and I didn't even want to do it. I wonder if the guy Cal hit wanted to fight. He hurt Cal's girlfriend. I wonder if she was mad, too.

"Is that why you and Jenny broke up?" I blurt out.

Pause. "What?"

"The girl in the picture. You called her Jenny when I brought you those waffles. Did you guys break up because of the fight? Was she mad at you for it?"

Cal glances in the rearview mirror, then back at the road. "Yeah, Jenny was mad, but honestly, it's none of your business. You gotta respect my boundaries, man."

"Sorry."

"Don't be sorry. Just stay out of my personal life, okay?"

"I just wanted to know what happened."

He lets out a slow breath, just like Mom. "We were good together. I messed it up. The end."

I wait for Cal to say something else, but he doesn't.

We park the supervan beside the bakery and go inside with Cal's finish samples. He has little square wood chips glued to a board that show a dozen different colors and levels of shine. Some are dull, like the wood on our front porch, and others are shiny as an ice cube.

Mr. Bovella is worried about picking the wrong color.

"That's the great thing about working with solid wood," Cal tells him. "Most furniture is a veneer finish—a thin ply of hardwood over particle board, so you can't sand it down, but with this wood, we can. So, let's pick your top three finishes and I'll do some big test pieces."

Mr. Bovella smiles. He seems relieved that his furniture isn't fake. I don't blame him. The idea of hiding cheap stuff behind a thin piece of real wood sounds pretty sneaky to me.

It's lunchtime, but the bakery isn't that busy. A girl I don't know is working the register. I glance at the swinging door to the kitchen for the thousandth time, and somehow, Sam is there.

"Sam?"

Mr. Bovella glances at the counter. "Sam stayed home from school today." He looks at me and actually smiles. "She assured me it was her choice to skip her shift Saturday, not yours."

The last thing I expected was a sort-of apology from Mr. Bovella. I'm so surprised I just sit there for a minute, wondering what Sam must have said to change his mind.

Cal nudges me. "Why don't you go talk to your friend. I'll get you when we're done."

I get up from the table and walk over to the counter slowly, hoping that Cal won't tell Mr. Bovella I got suspended for fighting. That would not go over well.

Sam watches me with a flat expression. I can't tell if she's mad at me or not, but when I get to the counter, she tips her head for me to follow and goes through the swinging door.

I step into the back with my heart beating a little harder. What I find is an assembly line of people packing boxes with cookies of all kinds.

"We have a huge birthday party this afternoon," Sam says, and I breathe a sigh of relief that she doesn't seem to be angry—until I see her brother standing at the end of the line.

Panic rushes through me. "What is Luca doing here?"

"It's his travel period," Sam says. "He stopped by to help us, but I guess it's time to do this." She takes a deep breath. "Luca, can I talk to you for a minute?"

Sam's brother looks up with a smile, which vanishes as soon as he sees me standing next to her. He glances around like he's considering making a break for it.

Sam walks over and takes his arm. "Let's go outside," she says.

I follow them to a door on the far side of the room.

As soon as the door clicks shut behind us, Luca turns on me. "What is wrong with you? Why did you have to drag my little sister into this?"

Heat flashes through me. "Why doesn't Jared want me talking to the Dog Lady?"

"I have no idea," Luca says.

"Then why did Joey attack me?"

"Joey attacked you?" Sam says.

"Yeah. At school, after you left. I'm suspended. That's why I'm here. Joey said Jared saw us talking to the Dog Lady. He warned me to stop prying into things."

A look of horror crosses Sam's face. "Luca, what's going on? I've been trying really hard to believe you, but this is ridiculous. Are you lying about what happened to Will?"

Luca looks up at the sky, his fists clenched. "Why can't you just leave it alone?"

"Luca," Sam says. "You know I can't do that."

Luca looks at me again. His jaw twitches.

I ask him the same question I asked Sam. "You know CPR, right?"

Luca's face crumbles. He nods.

"There was water in Will's lungs," I said. "Someone did CPR on him. I saw the bruises."

"I didn't know the kid hit his head—" Luca's voice breaks. Tears shine at the corners of his eyes. "I should've jumped in sooner. I should've gone right in after him."

"Oh my god," Sam says. "What happened? Please just tell us."

"He tripped," Luca says, and my blood runs cold. "Will fell into the pit and landed in the water. Yes, I did CPR. What else was I supposed to do? I wasn't going to let him die."

Sam covers her face with her hands. Her shoulders shake.

"I'm sorry, Sammy," Luca says. "I'm so sorry."

None of this makes any sense.

"Will just tripped?" I ask. "Jared didn't do anything to him?"

Luca wipes his tears away. "Jared tossed Will the bottle, but he caught it fine. Will walked over to the pit with it and tripped. Fell in head-first. I should have known he might have a head injury. We train for that at the pool. It all happened so fast."

"You told the police that Will left the roundhouse. You said he tried to follow me."

"I'm sorry," Luca says. "He didn't."

I can't feel anything.

My whole body has gone numb.

Will never left the roundhouse. He didn't even *try* to follow me.

"Luca, how could you?" Sam says through her tears.

"I'm sorry," Luca says. "I got him out of the water, got his airway clear. He was breathing, but he just wouldn't wake up. I took Joey home. Jared said he would deal with Will."

They told everyone that Will tried to follow me, but that isn't what happened.

It was an accident, and they tried to cover it up.

Red hot resolve pours through my veins. "What happened after you did CPR?"

"We carried Will to Jared's car," Luca says. "Jared was going to take him to the hospital. I'm so sorry, Sam. I never should have taken them to the Res with us."

"We have to tell the police," Sam says.

Luca nods. Fresh tears run down his cheeks.

The police. Yellow tape. We saw it at the roundhouse. But also on Brookside Drive.

"Wait!" They both look at me. "If Jared was taking Will to the hospital, how did Will end up by the side of the road?"

"I don't know," Luca says. "I really don't."

23
FALLOUT

FRIDAY MORNING BREAKS CLEAR and colder than it's been so far this fall. As soon as the daylight hits my eyes, I'm awake. I cram my feet into my slippers and head straight downstairs. Dad's at the stove, making his famous stuffed waffles with our waffle maker.

Mom's at the kitchen table. "No change," she says, and my heart dips. The longer Will stays in a coma, the less chance there is for him to wake up. The doctors keep saying his brain function looks really good and they don't understand why he hasn't woken up yet. It could be that his brain needs a little more time. It could be that something's wrong.

They don't know.

None of us knows.

I can't stop thinking about what Luca said at the bakery.

Jared said he was taking Will to the hospital, but the Dog Lady found Will on Brookside Drive. What did Jared do, drive to the other side of the Res and dump Will by the side of the road like a bag of trash?

I grab some juice and drop into the chair next to Shelley.

"Hey, bruiser," she jokes. I flick a crumb from the table at her, and she throws her hands up. "Watch the hair! Some of us have to go to school."

"Imagine being bad at school," I say.

"You're so weird," she says, but she's smiling.

"How are you feeling?" Mom asks. "I can't believe what Luca did. I'm glad Cal was there with you. Do you want me to see if Dr. Williamson can fit you in today?"

"I'm okay."

Now that we know the other boys lied, I should feel better. But I don't. They lied, all of them. Even Joey. They told me Will tried to follow me, but he didn't. Will fell in on his own, when he could have left. He didn't even try to come after me. He stayed with them, which should make me feel better, because it isn't all my fault that Will got hurt.

A tiny voice in the back of my head whispers that maybe it's *Will's* fault he got hurt.

Which means I'm blaming my friend for his own coma.

That cold, slimy feeling washes over me.

"Waffle up," Dad says, sliding a plate with a sausage, egg, and cheese stuffed waffle in front of me. Shelley passes the syrup and I drown every square.

"I'm heading out," she says, pushing back from the table. She pauses to ruffle my hair. "Keep your chin up, little bro. It's going to be okay."

I look up in surprise and she gives me a noogie before saying her goodbyes and leaving.

"Did you hear back from Frank?" Mom asks Dad.

"He hasn't returned my calls." Dad looks at me. "Do me a favor and stick close to the house, okay? We don't need any more confrontations with the Petersons right now."

Cal walks into the kitchen and plucks a chunk of waffle off my plate.

"Hey!"

He shamelessly stuffs the whole chunk in his mouth. "Sowwy, kid."

Mom smiles. "You never did have any patience," she says, and for once she's not mad.

Cal grabs the orange juice from the fridge and winks at me. "Don't worry, you can have part of mine. Speaking of which, could you help me with this fancy waffle contraption, Tim?"

Dad laughs and gets up to make Cal a waffle.

"Remember how we did Christmas presents?" Mom asks, and Cal nods.

"Yeah. In a circle."

I take a bite of my waffle and syrup runs down my chin. "Why a circle?"

Mom looks at Cal, and he says, "Go for it."

"Your grandma liked to take turns opening presents," Mom says. "On Christmas morning, we passed out the gifts and sat in a circle. Each person opened one gift at a time until they were all gone. We used to try to make it last as long as possible."

"You remember that marble chute game?" Cal says. "She wrapped it in, like, ten different pieces so it took longer to open. Weird shapes, too. No idea how she did it."

"Mom was good with her hands," Mom says, her voice soft for a moment. "Anyway, I always tried to be the last one with a present, but your uncle here had a different strategy."

"I opened everything."

I almost choke on my waffle. "What?"

"He opened everything ahead of time and tried to put the wrapping back," Mom says, "but one year he got the labels mixed up."

Cal cracks up. "You should've seen the look on Dad's

face when he opened that set of training bras that was supposed to be for you. It was totally worth it."

"Oh my god," Mom says, covering her face while she laughs. "Why did she buy those?"

"You know why," Cal says, and Mom shrieks.

For a minute, they look like two people who really get along. I wonder why they can't be like that all the time. Is Mom really that mad about the fight Cal got into? She's always acting like he's reckless and wild, but he works so hard and lets me help him all the time.

"Why do you guys fight so much?"

Mom frowns at her coffee. "We don't."

"Yes, we do," Cal says, and they are right back to giving each other the stink eye.

Mom's phone rings. She checks the number. "Detective Sherman," she says, and glances at Dad before answering. She walks out of the room with the phone on her ear.

Cal watches her go. His brow furrows. "The stuff's hitting the fan, huh?"

"Yeah."

Dad sets a fresh waffle in front of Cal. "Everything's going to be okay," Dad says, but he's watching the door Mom went through as hard as we are.

An eternity later, Mom finally walks back into the kitchen. "That was a courtesy call. Detective Sherman is stopping by in a few minutes with some questions for you, Max."

My skin runs cold.

"I'd better make myself scarce," Cal says, and Mom nods.

He starts to walk out of the room, and my heart lurches. I don't want him to leave.

"Can you stay?" I ask, and Cal stops.

"It's your funeral," Mom says. They engage in some kind of silent staring battle, which Cal apparently wins, because he plops back into his chair at the table.

"Sure, kid," he says. "I'll stay."

Mom cleans when she's stressed out. She says she can't help it. When things feel out of control, she goes around picking up socks and straightening drawers until she feels better. I kind of wish that was my reaction, too. It would sure make doing my chores easier. Instead, I usually start playing video games and forget to clean my room. There are only so many alarms you can put on your phone, and no one's perfect at OHIO, no matter how hard you try.

By the time Detective Sherman arrives, Mom has vacuumed the living room and dusted the tables, and me and Cal and Dad have managed to stay out of her way.

The detective walks in with a warm greeting for all of us. "Nice to see you again, Mr. Nichols," she says to Cal.

His eyebrows go up. "Wow. Good memory."

Detective Sherman taps the side of her head and takes a seat. "Hello, Max," she says as she opens her little flip pad. "How are you doing?"

"I'm okay."

"I hear you had a conversation with Samantha and Luca Bovella yesterday. I just want to confirm a few of those details with you, if that's all right."

I nod. There's a knot forming in my throat.

"According to Luca Bovella, Will Schwartz did not leave the roundhouse to follow you home as previously stated. Instead, Will was injured when he fell into the water and Luca administered CPR to revive him. Is that consistent with what he stated to you?"

"Yes."

"Luca stated that they carried Will Schwartz to Jared

Peterson's car, and at that point Luca Bovella left the scene. Did you happen to witness any of this activity?"

"No."

"I understand you had an altercation with Joey Peterson at school and received a suspension. Did Joey comment on the incident involving Will Schwartz during this time?"

"No. He just said Jared made him fight me."

"I see." She writes something down. "Did Joey state why his brother gave this directive?"

"Because I was talking to our neighbor, Ms. Barrington."

"And what were you talking to your neighbor about?"

I glance at Mom, and she nods that's it's okay. Dad smiles encouragement.

"Me and Samantha Bovella have been trying to figure out what happened to Will."

Detective Sherman gives me a long look. "Did you visit the crime scene by chance?"

"Yeah. We went to the roundhouse and Brookside Drive."

"Max," Mom says, because this information is new to her, too.

Detective Sherman leans forward, her elbows on her knees. "I understand you want to help your friend, Max. We all do. However, I have to ask that you leave the investigating to me. The last thing we want is for someone else to get hurt."

"Understood," Mom says.

Cal shakes his head. "Seems to me like the kid's been helpful. Just saying." Mom cuts her eyes at him, and he adds, "What? It's true!"

"That is true," Detective Sherman says, "and we thank you for your cooperation, Max."

"What happens now?" Dad asks. "Are these older boys going to be held accountable?"

Detective Sherman closes her flip pad. "Unfortunately, we have conflicting accounts of the incident. Jared and Joey Peterson maintain that their original statements are accurate."

My face flushes hot. "But Luca said Will stayed at the roundhouse. He said so."

"I believe that may be true," Detective Sherman says. "We found Will's glasses in the water there this morning. He may have lost them when he fell."

Mom covers her mouth with her hand and Dad wraps an arm around her.

Cal blows out a breath. "Damn." He looks at me. "Excuse my French."

I imagine Will falling into that pit of black water and wish I had never heard of the roundhouse, and that we had never spent the night at Joey's house. There are so many things I would take back. So many choices that would have changed everything.

But I can't go back. I have to find a way forward.

The dogs barking. My heart pounding. The light coming on. Upstairs, then downstairs.

"The Dog Lady is lying," I blurt out.

Detective Sherman raises her eyebrows and Mom says, "Ms. Barrington, our neighbor."

"Did you speak to Ms. Barrington?" the detective asks me.

"Me and Sam pretended we were doing an interview. Ms. Barrington said she wasn't home that night, but I remembered that I saw her lights come on. I saw a shadow in the window. I think she was there."

"Do you recall what time that was, approximately?"

"Sam said it was three a.m."

"Did you happen to look at your phone or a clock when you got home?"

I shake my head. I feel terrible. Why didn't I look at the time when I got home?

"Thank you, Max. Is there anything else you'd like to share?"

Other than the Dog Lady lying, all I have left is Jared. Jared may not have hurt Will on purpose, but he tried to cover it up. Who knows what else he did?

"Jared said he was taking Will to the hospital. How did Will end up in Brookside Drive?"

"I can't speak to that yet," Detective Sherman says, "but I intend to find out."

24

CAUSE AND EFFECT

OUR LATEST ASSIGNMENT FOR our writing note-books is to create a story spine for the books we've been reading. I'm not going back to school until Monday, but Ms. Little sent the directions by e-mail so I can stay caught up while I'm suspended. The story spine is a road map for the story, made of causes and effects. A cause is an event that makes something happen. An effect is what happens because of the cause.

There are words that connect these ideas.

Because.

If. Then.

Ms. Little's story spine has blanks for us to fill in. At first the character's world is normal, but then it changes. Because of that, something else happens. And on, and on.

Saturday morning, I turn on some music to help me focus and write down three facts.

Will, on the side of the road.

His glasses, in the roundhouse.

The Dog Lady and Jared, both lying.

For all of these things to be true, they have to be connected somehow. But which are the causes, and which are the effects? Detective Sherman said to leave the investigating to her, but these are my friends. I know them. She might not be able to get Joey to tell the truth, but I probably can. It doesn't matter if Jared is scary. I have to get Joey to talk to me again.

I stare at the page until my stomach growls, then I give up and go downstairs for breakfast. The rest of the family is already there. I look at Mom and she shakes her head. No change. She hands me a bowl of oatmeal and I drop into the only open chair at the table.

Dad and Cal are hunched over Cal's notes for the display cases.

"You know what you need?" Dad says. "An inventory system. I bet we could RFID-tag each piece of furniture and track it in a spreadsheet."

Cal puts up a hand. "Whoa, there. This is a no-spreadsheet zone."

They laugh, and Dad says, "If you change your mind, I have plenty of free time."

"Did you hear from the granola people?" I ask, and Dad shakes his head.

"No news yet."

Shelley crosses her fingers on both hands. "You got this, Dad."

"I hope so," he says, but he looks less than certain.

Mom walks over from doing the dishes and rubs Dad's shoulders. "If you're free, then you can go with us to meet the college application consultant this afternoon."

"Wow. Is that a thing?" Cal says.

"Yes," Mom says, with an edge to her voice. "You may have dropped out, but some of us appreciate the opportunity to go to college." She says it half under her breath, but we all hear it.

I feel like I just got in trouble again, even though she's talking about Cal, not me.

Cal's face goes still. "Okay, then." He grabs his stuff and walks out.

Mom sighs.

"Do you really have to give him such a hard time?" Dad says.

"Me? You're kidding, right?"

"Have it your way, Em. Just don't complain when he

leaves and never comes back." Dad flexes his fingers. "Now about this college consultant. How much is this going to cost?"

Mom, Dad, and Shelley start talking college, so I swallow down the rest of my oatmeal and head outside to find Cal. He's sitting in the driver's seat of the supervan, blasting music with a very loud guitar solo. The volume's so loud his broken window is vibrating.

I wave to get his attention, and he turns the music down. The Dog Lady's dogs are absolutely losing it.

"What do you say we get out of here?" he says.

He doesn't have to ask me twice.

I text Mom on the way to Bovella's. Cal has finished three big boards with the colors Mr. Bovella liked last time. Mr. Bovella chooses one of them, and we're off to the hardware store to buy the stain. The assembled display cases are waiting in our garage, ready to be finished.

The whole time we were at the bakery, I kept hoping to see Sam, but she and Luca weren't around. And to be honest, Mr. Bovella didn't seem too happy to see me again.

Which sucks.

I haven't heard from Sam since Luca's confession. I don't

know how I'm going to do this without her. Joey won't talk to me. Jared probably wants to kill me. And Will is still not awake.

In the hardware store, I feel like everyone is staring at me, even though I know they're not. When we climb back into the supervan, Cal asks where my can is, and I realize I left it on the counter. He goes back inside to get it while I sit there and wish I could remember things like a normal person. This knot starts to form in my throat, and suddenly it's so much pressure that I can't stop the tears. They start pouring from my eyes like a faucet that's been turned on.

Cal hops back into the supervan. His face goes soft when he sees me. "Hey, kid." Hearing his voice all gentle makes me cry even harder. He pats my shoulder. "It's okay, man. Let it out."

The tears flow until my nose is stopped up. Cal pats my back while I get through it. The hiccups fade, and he hands me a crumpled tissue. I blow my nose until I can breathe again.

"Better?" Cal asks, and I shrug. I do feel better, but also a little ashamed for losing it.

"Sorry for all the snot."

"It's no problem."

"I can't even remember a freaking paint can." Tears threaten again.

Cal squeezes my shoulder. "It's okay, man. I forget stuff

all the time. I had a pair of sneakers when I headed out here, but I left them at this campsite I stopped at. Or maybe I never brought them." He laughs. "I'm allergic to organization. Nothing I can do about it, been that way my whole life. All you can do is be yourself. You gotta embrace the weird, man."

I say the words back to myself in my head, and my brain shows me this pattern. It's the DNA strands we looked at in science. They twist around one another, with all these tiny bridges in between, connecting them. There is a pattern here. Cal spaces out. He forgets things. His handwriting is so terrible Mom made him redo his homework, and when she yells at him . . . it feels like she's talking to *me*.

He's so much like me.

"Do you have ADHD?" I blurt out.

Cal laughs as if I'm joking, but I'm not. When Dr. W asked Mom if we had any family members with ADHD, Mom had said no. But maybe she's wrong about that.

By now, Cal's noticed that I'm not laughing. "You're serious?" he says.

"You space out. You lose things. You didn't like school."

"No, I liked school," he says. "I just wasn't very good at it."

"But you're really smart. You make this furniture—"

"Eh, that's called earning a living."

He's blowing me off so hard I'm mad. "Is there something wrong with having ADHD?"

"No, of course not," he says. "They just didn't test for that stuff when I was a kid. I've always been a little different, but I never thought . . ." He stares out the windshield.

"Trailing off your sentences is a sign of ADHD. My therapist says so."

Cal looks over at me. "Thanks, Max. You're, uh, not the first person to bring this up."

"Mom?"

"No. My girlfriend, Jenny." He sighs. "She wanted me to get tested, but I thought I was already this old, what can it matter? I let her down too many times. The fight was the last straw."

"Can't you apologize or something?"

He frowns. "She doesn't want to hear from me."

"How do you know that?"

"I guess I don't," Cal says. "You know what, Max? You're a lot more grown up than I thought you were. And I don't just mean that your feet can reach the pedals." He winks, and a weird look comes over his face. "You know what we need right now?"

"What?"

He grins. "Driving lessons."

25
BLIND SPOTS

CAL LEANS OVER FROM the passenger seat and fixes my hand placement on the supervan's steering wheel. "Whatever you do, don't let go. Okay? And keep your foot on the brake."

"Okay." My feet reach the pedals no problem. The issue is that I know we shouldn't be doing this, but I can't resist. I feel like I'm on top of a mountain, ready to fly off.

We're sitting in the empty school parking lot behind the middle school. I never come here on the weekends, so it looks strange without any cars or kids around.

This is the best or worst idea Cal has ever had.

I can't decide yet.

"The important thing to remember is, she won't move fast," he says. "It takes a lot of gas to get this beast going.

When you start her up, we'll just sit here with the parking brake on. That's this lever over here by your left knee." He reaches across me to point at a handle under the dash. "The brake is on now, so she won't go anywhere. Promise."

"Okay."

"Now turn the key."

I grip the key to the right of the wheel and crank it. The engine whines for a second before it roars to life. The supervan has always been a little loud and startling, with the backfiring and everything, but sitting in the driver's seat, it feels like I'm strapped to a rocket.

"That's it," Cal says with a grin.

"You know I'm only eleven, right?"

"Twelve soon, though."

"In October."

"Ah." He laughs. "Close enough!"

Cal starts pointing out the different parts of the steering wheel. There's a lever that puts the van into drive or reverse. The wheel itself is skinny, covered in hard brown leather with ridges. It feels like one of those rhythm sticks from music class. There's a knob that sticks up from the wheel to help with turning, which Cal uses to whip us around corners. The more I learn, the better I feel.

"Can we take the parking brake off?"

"Sure," Cal says. "Let's just practice rolling her forward. There's no one here, but always check your mirrors before moving." He shows me how to check my blind spots to make sure there aren't any obstacles I can't see using the mirrors. "Make sure you look last where you'll get hit first. Now put your foot on the brake and pull the parking lever to release the parking brake."

I do what he says and the supervan starts to roll forward, so I press the brake pedal.

"Good! That's good. Now just let up on the brake a little."

I do, and the van rolls forward. We are going two miles per hour, but my heart is racing.

"And stop."

We do this over and over, just using the brake, no gas. I steer the van to the left, and we complete a half circle before the lot turns uphill and the van stops rolling.

"Well done," Cal says. "Now, when you put your foot on the gas, I want you to imagine you're tapping your toes. Not stepping with all of your weight. Just a gentle toe tap."

I press the gas and the engine roars, but the van barely goes anywhere. I'd really have to mash my foot down to fly up this hill. I try a little more gas, and we get rolling, though I can't help stomping on the brake every time we start to speed up. We keep going like that for a while, until it's getting late enough that Mom texts me wondering where we are.

"Shoot! We have to go home," I tell Cal.

He sighs. Looks at me. "Want to drive her there?"

"Isn't that illegal?"

"Probably."

I know this isn't the smartest decision, but I'm feeling pretty full of myself after doing doughnuts in the parking lot for an hour, and we're only three turns from home.

We go so slowly I'm sure we'll get honked at, but miraculously we don't pass many cars. I'm staring so hard at the road and checking all the mirrors so much that Cal has to remind me to use the gas a few times, but somehow, we inch our way onto my street.

I aim the van at the open curb in front of our house and can't believe I did this.

Then something moves in front of Joey's house.

My foot presses the brake, but the supervan takes off.

"Hit the brake," Cal says, and I press harder, but the van just zooms down our street.

"The brake, the brake!" Cal shouts, but I'm frozen.

He dives across me for the parking brake, which yanks the steering wheel to the side. The van swerves. He pulls the lever as the tires hit the curb. We bounce into the air and slam into something with a horrible crunch. My body flies forward but the seat belt yanks me back.

The van lurches to a stop.

Cal pries himself upright and turns the ignition off. The van goes quiet except for a ticking noise from the engine. We're face-to-face with the maple tree on the berm in front of the Dog Lady's house. The van's hood is tight against the tree's trunk. One of the lower branches is smashed against the windshield. Her dogs are absolutely losing their minds.

"Well, that didn't go exactly as planned," Cal says.

I look down and realize I was pushing the gas pedal instead of the brake. I expect to see steam or flames rising from the engine, but the van looks totally normal from this angle. I can't tell if there's any damage, other than the broken branches on the Dog Lady's tree. "I wrecked your van."

"It'll be all right."

I remember what Cal said about looking last where you'll get hit first. "I forgot to look at the trees," I say, which is ridiculous, but it's all my brain can offer right now.

Cal busts out laughing. "You're okay, kid. It's okay."

At first, I think he's right.

Then I hear Mom's voice.

"Max!" She appears in the passenger side window and yanks the door open. She's breathing hard, her face red and her eyes wet. When she sees Cal in the passenger seat and me on the driver's side, she shrieks. "How dare you! He's my *son*, Cal!"

"Mom, I'm okay," I say, but she ignores me. I unclip my seat belt and jump out.

Mom's yelling at Cal as I run around to the passenger side. "This is why I can't trust you," she shouts. "Why can't you act like a responsible adult?"

"Mom," I say, and she finally looks at me long enough to realize I'm right there. She flings her arms around me and hugs me tight while Cal climbs out of the van.

"See, he's okay," Cal says.

Mom turns to face him. "You have no idea what it's like to put someone else's life before your own. Who made sure you did your homework? *Me.* Who got you to school on time? *Me.* I did it. You never had to worry about anything because I worried for you."

"I didn't ask you to," Cal says.

"I didn't have a choice! Our parents weren't there! I was nineteen." Mom's crying, thick tears tracing her cheeks. "I didn't even get to finish college and you *dropped out*."

"Mom, wait—" I'm trying to get her to stop long enough to hear me.

Dad comes running into the street with Shelley on his heels. "Is everyone okay?"

"What happened?" Shelley says, as she gives me a quick hug.

"I grew up, Em," Cal says. "I'm not that same scared kid anymore."

"Max could have been *killed*," Mom says.

"He seems okay," Dad says.

Mom blows him off. "You didn't have to go to the hospital and identify your own parents."

"Mom!" I shout. I can see it now: Cal and I are so alike. "He's just like me, Mom."

"It's okay, kid," Cal says. "You don't have to defend me."

"No, it's not okay! Mom, remember what Dr. Williamson said about genetics? Cal's my uncle. He lost his sneakers. He has bad handwriting!"

"Max—"

"It was both of us, Mom. We both did the driving lesson, and I know we shouldn't—"

"Your uncle's an *adult*," Mom says.

"So, I can make mistakes, but he can't?"

"He's violating his *parole*!" Mom shouts.

Everything stops.

Cal blows out a long breath.

I stare at him in shock. "You're on parole?"

"Suspended sentence," he says. "I'm not supposed to leave Arizona."

So that's why he hasn't visited. He *couldn't*. I feel like I'm looking at a stranger again.

"Oh my god," Shelley says.

The full weight of what Cal said settles onto my heart. He lied to me. He said he came here to help us, but he was really running away from his own problems.

"Come on, let's go inside," Dad says. He wraps an arm around Mom and turns her toward the house. Her head dips to his side. "Shelley. Max. Let's go."

I linger for a second. I still can't believe what I just heard. Cal's the one who keeps telling me to live my truth. To be myself. But who is he?

"Why didn't you tell me?" I ask.

"I'm sorry." Cal sighs. "No one's perfect, kid."

"Max!" Dad calls.

"Go on," Cal says. "Your family needs you."

I turn away and leave him standing there alone.

26
HERE GOES NOTHING

SHELLEY IS ONLY FIVE years older than me, but it feels more like a decade sometimes, especially when I just wrecked my uncle's van. She's a straight-A student. I'm not. She's organized. I'm not. She doesn't need ten thousand alarms, a launch pad, and OHIO to do things right.

When I was little, Shelley had this toy kitchen in her room. I had to sit there forever while she poured imaginary tea, adding milk, sugar, and plastic lemon wedges until it was perfect. This is what I think of while she fixes me a hot chocolate after the wreck.

She measures Dad's famous dry hot chocolate mix with an actual measuring spoon and stirs until all the lumps are gone. "Want marshmallows?" she asks.

"Yeah."

"Whipped cream?"

I'm so tired. "I don't care."

She purses her lips. "How can you not care about your own hot chocolate?" she says.

"It's more exhausting to think about it than to do whatever."

She stares at me for a long moment and plops a few mini marshmallows on top of my hot chocolate. Then she opens the fridge and grabs a jar of pickles.

"What are you doing?"

"Don't worry about it," she says with an evil grin. She unscrews the lid.

"I don't want pickles."

"I thought you said you didn't care?"

My forehead drops against the table with a thunk.

She laughs. "Okay, okay, here you go."

The mug lands next to my face. I sit up. Shelley's playing it cool, but she keeps glancing in the direction of the stairs. Mom and Dad went up there to talk. Cal's still outside in the supervan, which is parked in front of our house again. From what I can see through the window, the front doesn't even look that smashed. The big metal bumper must have helped.

"I can't believe you drove Uncle Cal's van," Shelley says.

I rest my forehead on the table again and groan.

"I bet Mom and Dad are going to make you work off the cost of the repairs."

"Stop."

Shelley pokes my arm. "Ooh, maybe you'll have to mow the Dog Lady's lawn to make it up to her. Her tree is pretty messed up."

I groan again. I feel terrible. Ms. Barrington isn't the friendliest neighbor, but she never did anything to me. I should probably go apologize. Dr. W is always saying that I need to work on apologizing to others and forgiving myself, even if other people don't, but it's not easy.

"What were you thinking?" Shelley asks. "I just started driver's ed this year, and Dad still won't let me practice in the minivan. He says I have to get my permit first."

I peek up at her. "I don't know, it sounded fun."

She smirks. "You're so grounded."

"Imagine being grounded."

She laughs. "Oh, I've been grounded."

I sit up. "No, you haven't."

"Uh, yes I have. You just don't remember because you were still a little terror in training. Let's see," she pauses, counting,

"I was in eighth grade, so you were in third. You would have been, like, eight or nine years old." She counts again. "Yeah, you were eight, because it happened right at the beginning of the school year. Gosh, I *hated* that history teacher."

"What happened?"

"I cheated, and I got in huge trouble for it."

My jaw hits the floor. "No, you didn't."

"Uh, yes I *did*." She makes a face. "School gets harder in eighth grade. They're, like, getting you ready for high school. I had this history teacher who gave us these paragraph essays every week, and we had to read part of the textbook to answer them. I swear, reading history books makes me fall asleep. So. *Boring*."

"But you love school."

She shrugs. "I love getting good grades, but I don't love every single one of my classes. That history teacher was the worst. No matter what I wrote, he picked out little mistakes and marked me down. I could never get an A. So, a few weeks into school, I just copied something from online. I wanted to see if I could get a better grade, or if he'd mark that up, too."

I can't believe it. "What did he do?"

"He ran it through a plagiarism app or something and found it online. He gave me a zero. Mom and Dad were *not* happy."

My mind is blown. "Who *are* you even?"

Shelley laughs again. "I've done plenty of ill-advised things."

"I guess I thought school was always easy for you."

She goes over to her bag and gets a textbook, then opens it in front of me so I can see all the highlighting and notes she's made. "Does that look easy?"

I shake my head. I could never spend that long working on my notes.

"This is what I'm good at," Shelley says. "Just like you're good at art and using the 3D printer and creative stuff like that. I love school, but it's still hard work. Sometimes I wish I could care less like some of my friends, but I like getting A's too much."

"I don't have to worry about getting A's."

"That's nonsense," she says. "You can be a straight-A student, Max. I mean, school is harder with ADHD. That's a fact, but that's what your accommodations are for. And meds, if you need them. You wouldn't go around without insulin if you had diabetes, right?"

She closes her book and sets it on the table, on top of a pile of brochures for different colleges. I think about her going away and feel a sudden heaviness in my chest.

"What did the college person say?"

"I've got a chance at scholarships, but I have to keep my grades up. It's hard to get into the big colleges in New York, Boston, or Chicago. I have a lot of work to do."

"Same."

She smiles. "I wish I was an artist like you. I can't draw a straight line to save my life."

"Really?"

"Yes, really. You're so full of ideas. Sometimes I feel like all I can do is read other people's words and regurgitate what they want me to say." She glances at me. "That means—"

"Barfing. I know."

We giggle at that. I always thought Shelley was some kind of super brain, but maybe she's just doing what she's good at. That doesn't mean she's smarter than me, or that she doesn't work hard. It feels like there's a future where I can understand her again, just in a new way.

She picks a marshmallow out of her cocoa and flings it at me. It hits me square in the forehead and I slump back over my chair, pretending to be dead.

Dad walks into the kitchen. He pauses when he sees us. "Everything okay?"

I sit up fast.

"Yeah, we're good," Shelley says.

"I'm going to see if Cal needs any help with the van," Dad says. "Back soon."

A few minutes later, Mom walks into the kitchen. Her hair is wrapped in a towel. She's wearing her fluffy pink bathrobe, the one Dad gave her for Christmas as a joke, but which she insists on wearing because it makes her feel like the Energizer Bunny.

"You okay?" Shelley asks, and for a second, she sounds the way they do. Like an adult.

Mom smiles at both of us. "Sorry I lost it out there. Max, don't ever do that again, okay? I really need you to understand how dangerous that was."

"I'm sorry, Mom."

"I know you are," she says, "but you're also grounded. Again."

"I was thinking I should go apologize to Ms. Barrington."

"That's a good idea," Mom says, and I jump up. "Wait, Max." I turn back. "What were you saying out there, about handwriting and sneakers?"

"Oh. I think Uncle Cal has ADHD."

Mom's mouth falls open, and then I'm out the door.

The Dog Lady's house is quiet when I get there. The tree isn't as bad as I thought, but there are still two broken branches hanging down. The trunk is a little ripped up in a couple of spots, too. I wonder if they make Band-Aids for trees. That's probably something Cal would know, but he and Dad seemed like they were having a serious talk when I passed by them in the supervan.

I look up at the Dog Lady's house. Here goes nothing.

This time I make it to her front porch without any dogs chasing after me. I ring the bell and a whole chorus of barks kicks up from inside. She must have them all in there.

A long minute goes by while I wait, until I finally see a shadow behind the curtained window next to the door. Her dogs quiet down.

I lean closer to the door. "Ms. Barrington? This is Max Greenberg, your neighbor. I came to apologize." My palms are sweaty. I wipe them on my jeans.

There's no response.

"I'm really sorry about your tree," I say.

Still nothing.

"Okay, I don't want to bother you, but I'm really sorry and we'll try to fix the tree."

It stinks to be ignored, but at least she's not setting her dogs on me. Maybe that counts for something.

I close her gate and walk back toward home. There's a charcoal smell in the air that makes my stomach rumble. Someone's cooking something. The closer I get to Joey's house, the more I'm sure the grilling smell is coming from their backyard.

I cut across Joey's lawn like I have a million times before and pop through the side gate in their fence. I don't even know if Joey's at his dad's or his mom's place today. I'm just thinking maybe if I tell him about everything Sam and I have done, he'll want to help. I can tell him about the Dog Lady. I can tell him about going to the hospital and seeing Will. There's no way he can hear that and keep lying. Will's our friend. I just have to remind Joey of that.

I round the corner of Joey's house.

Their grill comes into view.

And so does Jared.

27
SURVIVAL MODE

THERE ARE TWO POPULAR modes in my favorite video game, *Minecraft*: creative mode and survival mode. In creative mode, you're just mining blocks and building stuff and having fun, and none of the enemies can "nope" you. In survival mode, you have one goal: staying alive.

There's a reason I like creative mode the best.

In survival mode, I always die.

Jared stands there staring me down while my limbs go hot and fuzzy. It's adrenaline. *We learned about that in health class*, my brain spits out.

"What are you doing here?" Jared says. He's wearing a cutoff T-shirt that shows the muscles in his arms. The kitchen tongs in his hand look a lot more dangerous than they should, even though he's just standing in front of a grill covered in chicken pieces.

You can do this.

"I need to talk to Joey."

Jared shakes his head. "No can do."

"He's my friend."

Jared blows out a breath and takes a step toward me. "You shouldn't be here."

"I know." I'm trying to keep the tremble out of my voice. "I don't care." Because the truth is, I don't. I'm tired of playing these games. "I know you're lying about what happened at the roundhouse. Luca told me the truth. Will got hurt, and you covered it up."

Jared's blue eyes go icy. "You need to be very careful about what you say right now." He takes a step toward me. His biceps bunch as he squeezes the tongs.

"Did you dump Will by the side of the road?"

"No. What is wrong with you?" He glances at the house, then back to me. "If you keep running your mouth like this, you're going to end up in a world of hurt."

"Are you going to make Joey beat me up at school again? I know you made him do it."

Jared's gaze wavers. "I didn't tell him to hit you."

"Yeah, right."

He points at the gate. "You need to get out of here, kid."

A scorched smell hits my nose. "Is something burning?"

Jared glances at the grill, where the chicken is now smoking. "No, no, no." He rushes back to the grill. "Get out of here and stop distracting me!"

I decide to go for their back door while he's busy, but I only make it halfway across the patio before Jared leaps away from the grill and grabs my arm. "I said, get lost!"

A door slams inside their house, and I swear he jumps. "You have to go. *Now.*"

He shoves me so hard I almost fall. I stumble back, tripping over my big feet. I find my balance just when the sliding door starts to open.

"What's going on out here?" Mr. Peterson's voice booms.

Jared's in front of the grill, grabbing chicken off the flames as fast as he can. He glances at me, and it's not fury in his eyes. It's fear. That's when I see the pattern. Joey is scared of Jared, but Jared is scared of his father. He's in survival mode, too.

"You better not have messed it up again," Mr. Peterson says as he walks out onto the patio. He's only a little taller than me, but stocky. If Jared has fifty pounds on me, his dad has a hundred. His neck is as thick as my thigh.

"Idiot," Mr. Peterson mutters, as he snatches the tongs from Jared.

That's when I realize he's going to turn toward the grill and see me standing there like a deer in headlights. The last thing I see as I turn to run is Mr. Peterson grabbing Jared by the arm—the exact same way Jared did to me.

Early Sunday morning, I sneak down to the kitchen and make a huge tray of bacon. Extra crispy, just how Cal likes it. I'm hoping I can lure him back inside, seeing as he didn't come in for dinner last night. Mom said he needed some space, so we gave it to him.

When the bacon's ready, I pour a glass of OJ and jog outside, but the supervan is gone.

My heart skips a beat.

The curb is so empty without the van. Would Cal really leave without saying goodbye?

I look up the street. The Dog Lady's tree is all cleaned up. I go to check the time on my phone, but it's not in my pocket. I must have left it upstairs. Or in the kitchen. Who knows. I'm about to run inside to find it when a noise like something breaking comes from the garage.

The display cases.

Cal wouldn't leave without delivering those.

I run to the garage and fling the door open. The display cases are gone, but Dad is standing in the middle of the garage with a big panel of Styrofoam in his hands.

"Max," Dad says. He's panting. The floor is covered in broken chunks of Styrofoam. He lowers the panel in his hands and starts stacking the chunks.

"Where's Cal?"

"He decided it was best if he got going. We delivered the display cases earlier this morning."

My heart sinks. "Did you make him leave?"

"No, of course not."

"Is he coming back?"

"Probably not for a little while," Dad says as he stacks the last of the Styrofoam chunks. There are tiny white balls coating his arms and clothes. It looks like a snowman threw up all over him.

"What happened in here?"

Dad laughs, but it's not a happy sound. "I got a little carried away breaking down the Styrofoam to fit in the trash. I guess I just needed to blow off a little steam."

"But you're the rubber guy."

"The what?"

"You're like that saying, *I'm rubber and you're glue, whatever you say bounces off of me and sticks to you*," I say. "You never let anything bother you."

"Plenty of things bother me. I just try not to burden you all with it. I'm the one who's supposed to be taking care of you." He leans back against the storage racks along the side of the garage and rubs his hands over his face. "I got some bad news from the investors I met, and I guess I got a little angry about it. Those recipes were a real gamble, and it didn't pay off."

He looks over at me with this sad smile, as if he's letting me down. I may not know how to fix that problem, but I do know what my therapist would say.

"Dr. W says it's good to let your feelings out."

Dad's eyebrows go up. "You're right."

All this time, I thought Dad was just always happy, no matter what happened.

But he's not, just like me.

"How about we make a deal?" he says. "I'll spill my guts if you spill yours?"

A wave of emotion sweeps over me. "I think Joey's in trouble," I say, and Dad's face goes serious. "I mean, things seem bad at his house. I saw his dad yelling at Jared for burning some chicken and he was really angry."

Dad nods. "Thank you for telling me. That is not okay. I'll make sure to talk to Frank. I'll go over there this afternoon." He comes over and gives me a hug.

"Thanks, Dad."

"Anytime."

28
MUSCLE MEMORY

IT FEELS LIKE IT'S been a year since I saw Sam, but when I walk into class on Monday morning, she pops up like we haven't missed a beat. Her hair is pulled back into a ponytail like usual. She smiles, and I can't help smiling back. Sam smiles with her whole face.

"I've been thinking," she says, before I've even finished wedging myself under the kidney-shaped table we sit at. My mouth is dry and chalky, partly because I forgot to brush my teeth this morning, though I did manage a perfect pyramid with my waffles.

"Imagine not being able to think."

Sam shudders. "Ew."

"It could happen. You could turn into a zombie and only care about eating brains."

"I'd be the best zombie ever," Sam declares. "I'd eat the most brains."

We laugh as Ms. Little instructs everyone to get out our writer's notebooks. We're going to turn them in at the end of class so she can look at our story spines, if we want. Friday is our normal turn-in day, but I'm going to put mine in the bin today, too. I wrote a pretty cool story about a kid who finds an actual gem digging in his backyard. I'm thinking about how weird it is to look forward to sharing my writing when Sam taps my shoulder.

"I'm sorry I yelled at you about Luca," she says. "I didn't know he was lying."

"I get it. He's your brother."

"Yeah, I know, but facts are facts. You can't disagree with the truth." She sighs. I'm glad she's not mad at me, but I was the one who made Luca admit that he lied. That had to hurt.

"Luca told the truth," I say. "He went to the police. It was the right thing to do."

"Thanks," Sam says, but her smile is gone.

"I tried to talk to the Dog Lady yesterday."

Her face brightens. "What did she say?"

"Nothing. I was apologizing for running into her tree with Cal's van."

"Wait," Sam says. "You drove your funcle's van?"

"Yeah."

"This is why you need me around," she says, and I think that I really do. I missed having Sam there to share ideas and figure things out together.

"Can you come over today? Maybe we can try to talk to the Dog Lady again."

"I can't." She frowns. "My dad's picking me up."

"We'll figure something out," I say, but I'm not sure what.

We sit there listening as Ms. Little starts to read our daily picture book, but she barely gets started before the classroom phone rings. "One second," she says. She answers the phone, then hangs up and looks at me. And Joey. "Max. Joey. You two need to head to Ms. Chen's office."

I look at Sam and swallow. This can't be good.

Ms. Chen has three mandarin oranges lined up next to her pencil cup. They form a tiny line of defense along the front edge of her desk. A vitamin-C army.

"Hello, Max. Joey," she says. "I'd like to talk about your conflict last week and see if we can resolve whatever tension is occurring between you two."

I glance at Joey. He's picking at his nails.

"Joey, can you tell me what happened last week?" Ms. Chen asks.

"We got in a fight," he says. "Now we're in trouble."

She taps her pen. "I'm not a fan of punishing people for their mistakes. I'd rather get to the core of the problem and fix it. Does that sound good?"

Joey shrugs.

Ms. Chen switches to me. "Max, can you tell me what happened last week?"

I can, but I'd rather play UNO. "I was at my locker and Joey started hitting me with his bag full of books. I grabbed it to stop him, but I didn't hit him back."

"What were you feeling at the time?"

I'm about to say I was angry, but the knot in my stomach says something else. "I was upset. Sad, I guess. He's my friend. Or at least, he was until he ditched me."

Joey looks at me. "You quit the soccer team."

"What?"

"This summer," he says, his pale face going blotchy. "You ditched me first."

My neck goes hot. "I quit soccer because I was sick of getting carded all the time."

"Joey, have you been angry with Max all summer?" Ms. Chen asks.

Joey nods but doesn't say anything.

"Can you tell me how you're feeling right now?" she asks him.

"This isn't fair," Joey says. "Nothing's fair anymore."

"What else hasn't been fair?"

"My parents got divorced. My mom moved out. We have to switch places a lot and I'm always losing my stuff." He looks at me. "You and Will forgot about me."

It's the last thing I expected to hear. That *we* did something to *him*.

"No, we didn't."

"You never texted me when you were gaming," he says. "You said you would when I was at my mom's, but you never did."

"I forget things like that," I say, and somewhere in the back of my mind, I'm wondering what else I've forgotten. Is Joey right? Did I ditch him? Will and I hung out a lot over the summer, but that's because Will has a pool . . . and Joey wasn't there. Joey wasn't there, and when he was, he was always arguing with us and starting fights. And then it was Joey's birthday, so we went over to his house for his sleepover, and he convinced us to go to the Res.

He did that.

Ms. Chen nods at us. "This is good work. Thank you

for sharing, both of you. What needs to be done to make this right?"

I look down at the grimy friendship bracelet that's still around my wrist from this summer. Me and Will made them one afternoon when it was raining and we couldn't swim. Once upon a time, me and Joey and Will were best friends. Then Joey's parents got divorced. Because of that, Joey had to spend half his time at his mom's apartment. Because of that, he wasn't right there in front of me, and I forget things that aren't right in front of me. Because of that, he thought me and Will weren't his friends anymore. I didn't mean to ditch Joey this summer, but according to this story spine, maybe I did.

"I'm sorry," I say. "I didn't mean to ghost you. We just got busy playing, and I guess we forgot. I didn't do it on purpose. It sucked that you weren't there."

"You didn't act like it sucked," he says.

I remember all the afternoons spent in Will's pool. "I know."

Ms. Chen nods and says, "Joey, would you like to apologize to Max?"

"I'm sorry for coming after you in the hall," he says, and when he looks over at me, I can tell he means it. He's not just saying what she wants him to say.

When you learn a new skill in soccer, you have to do it a million times. That way your muscles remember what to do without you even thinking. It's called muscle memory, and I lost mine when my legs grew four inches over the summer. I still remember what it feels like to do certain moves, but my feet don't know where they are anymore.

I know how to be Joey's friend, though, even if we haven't been talking.

Even if things are changing.

"Imagine you broke your gaming hand," I say.

He grins. "Imagine no screens for a year."

"What is happening here?" Ms. Chen says, and we just laugh. She asks us a few more questions and tells us she'll be following up with each of us later this week. Joey gets a little quiet at that, and I wonder if he's going to tell her how things have been at home.

When Ms. Chen says we're done, we walk out into the hall together, which is weird for a moment. We both kind of glance at each other and look away.

"I saw that van crash yesterday," Joey says. "Were you driving it?"

"Yeah."

"That's so cool." He reaches out for a fist bump, like everything is totally normal between us. Like we're *fine*-fine. But we're not. I know, deep down, that Joey has to know the truth about what happened to Will. It's probably the whole reason he froze me out after Will got hurt, but this isn't about us being friends anymore. It's about Will.

"Luca told me what happened at the roundhouse," I say, and Joey's smile vanishes. "You have to tell the truth about the bottle, and Will falling into the pit, and everything."

His face drains of color. "I can't."

"Will's our *friend*. Friends don't lie."

Joey shakes his head, and all that hope I was feeling dries up. Just like that, we've forgotten how to be friends again. That's the tricky part about muscle memory. If you don't use it, you lose it. Go too long without touching a soccer ball and you won't remember how to do the skill at all. Apparently, the same rule applies to friendship.

"You can't keep lying forever," I say as Joey walks away.

His voice carries back to me. "I know."

29
NOBODY'S HERO

MOM HAS THE HOLE puncher out when I get home. The kitchen table is covered in papers and her slim blue real estate folders. She looks up when I walk in.

"I spoke to Will's mom this morning," she says. "He's been moving some. They don't know if the movement is involuntary or not, but it's something."

I dump my bag on the launch pad, grab a handful of cheese sticks from the fridge, and drop into the chair next to her. "Is involuntary bad?"

"Involuntary means he's not moving on purpose. The movements could be caused by random signals from his brain, like a finger twitch or a leg spasm, but Gina said he squeezed her hand. If he's responding to touch or words, that's a very good sign. How was school?"

"I got called to the social worker's office with Joey."

"How did it go?" Mom asks.

"He was mad at me and Will for forgetting him this summer."

"Oh," Mom says. "That had to be hard to hear."

You know how some things don't seem that bad until you think about them for a while? That's how I felt about what Joey said. At first, I was mad at him. For everything that happened with Will, but also for shutting me out. Then I found out why he was mad at me, and things made more sense, and for a while I was glad to just understand it better.

But now, after thinking about it all day, I feel worse.

Like I'm always going to mess everything up.

"Hey," Mom says, squeezing my wrist to bring me back. Her hand is warm on my skin. "Dad had a long talk with Joey's dad last night. Things have been rough since the divorce, but that's no excuse for Frank's behavior. Joey might be taking out his frustration on you."

"I forgot to text him. Like, a lot."

Another squeeze. "That doesn't mean you're a bad friend."

Doesn't it? If I can't remember to text my friends, can I even have friends? There's a heaviness gathering in my chest, like a cloud over my heart. I felt this way a lot last year, before the parent-teacher conference with my English teacher. It doesn't feel good.

"Let me show you something," Mom says. She opens her laptop and brings up her massive, color-coded calendar, which makes me groan. "Don't worry, this will be quick. Look at June sixteenth. That's when school ended."

"Joey told us his mom was moving out on the first day of summer."

"Yes," Mom says. "Now look at your therapy appointment for that week." She expands one of the color-coded bubbles and notes pop up. "You learned a lot of new things over the summer. You worked hard, but you couldn't do everything at once. At the beginning of the summer, you and Dr. Williamson were just starting to identify which strategies worked for you to remember things. You didn't even know about OHIO until much later in the summer. You can't blame yourself for what you didn't know."

Only Mom would remember this timing, thanks to her computer brain. A little bit of that cloud lifts off my heart, but it's still there, looming on the horizon.

"I wish I learned that stuff earlier."

Mom shuts her laptop. "Maybe we could have gotten you identified sooner, but we didn't, and I'm sorry for that. In my opinion, it's the world that expects too much of *you*.

You're brilliant. It's hard having ADHD in a neurotypical world. I've been thinking about that a lot, actually." She pauses. "I think you might be right about Cal."

She sighs. Straightens her folders. "He was always just so reckless, and we didn't have people like Dr. Williamson to help us. Back then, no one knew much about ADHD. It was still called ADD, and most people thought it was made up. Looking back, I can't believe I didn't see it. I was so hard on him." She blinks and blinks. "I let him blame himself all these years."

I look over at the fridge, half expecting to see Cal leaning against the counter drinking straight out of the orange juice carton, but he's not there.

"I miss him."

"Me too." Mom's smile falters. "I was just so focused on you, I didn't really consider what Dr. Williamson said, about ADHD running in families. Now I'm kind of wondering about myself, to be honest. I hope Cal will be open to getting tested. Maybe we can do it together."

"Will he come back when his probation is over?"

"I hope so," Mom says. "I left him a voice mail, but I really messed up this time."

She looks at me, and there's this moment where I don't recognize her. She's still my mom, but she's also different.

A mom who isn't a computer brain. A mom who makes mistakes and feels bad about them and wishes she had done things differently. A mom who isn't perfect, just like Shelley, and Dad . . . and *me*.

I'm sitting on the curb where the supervan used to be, wondering what I could text Cal to make him come back. It feels like there's something important I need to say to him. Yeah, he messed up with the driving lesson, but he also taught me so many things, about woodworking and family and staying cool when you feel super weird.

I keep typing words and deleting them. I wonder how far he's gotten. Is he halfway to Arizona by now?

I'm staring at my phone so hard I don't hear the dogs until they're almost on top of me. A snarl registers next to my ear and I jump up. It's the Dog Lady with her entire pack of dogs. "It's a good thing that horrid vehicle is gone," she says. "It was an eyesore."

"It wasn't that bad." She has no right to complain about Cal's supervan when her dogs make so much noise barking all the time.

"It's against town ordinance to park a recreational vehicle

at the curb for an extended period of time," she says, and I swear one of her dogs growls at me.

This is not helping the heavy feeling in my chest.

"Whatever. It's gone now."

She tugs on the leashes to pull the dogs back, and a long yellow line pops into the air at the exact same moment that a small, curly-haired dog breaks free of the pack.

"Charlotte!" she shouts, as the dog darts into the road.

I run into the street to grab the dog before it gets hit by a car. It's not that big, so I scoop it up and jog back to the curb. I don't know if it's a puppy or not, but the dog's fur is impossibly soft, which is surprising. I guess I expected everything to do with the Dog Lady to be a little rough.

The dog tries to lick my face as I step back onto the sidewalk. "Good boy," I say.

"She's a *she*," the Dog Lady corrects.

"Really? I just saved your dog," I say, and her lips go flat. She tosses me the leash while she holds the other dogs back. I clip the leash to the dog's collar and set it down. The dog jumps up, trying to lick me again, and I laugh.

"You're not scared of them," she says.

"I like dogs. I just don't like being barked at."

"They're dogs," she says. "What else are they supposed to do?" I pass the leash over to her, and she studies me for a long moment. "I must say, I'm surprised you'd care, after how you treated your friend."

"What do you mean?"

"Your friend in the hospital." I'm so busy thinking about dogs and leashes and Cal that it takes me a minute to realize she's talking about *Will*. "You're one of those boys that went into the woods," she says. "I saw what you said, in the papers. You said your friend got lost, but he didn't wander off on his own, now did he?"

Wander where? Into the woods? She must be talking about how she found him. "Will got hurt at the roundhouse," I say. "I don't know how he ended up on Brookside Drive."

"I took him to the hospital," she says. "What else was I supposed to do? They were going to blame my babies for what you boys did. I never asked for any of this hero nonsense." Her babies? What do her dogs have to do with Will? She's glaring at me so hard I can feel it on my skin, like I *did* something to her, but I didn't.

"I don't know what happened," I say. "I wasn't there. I got scared and left."

"Convenient," she mutters.

"It's not *convenient*. I should have been there. Will's my friend. He could have died!"

"You weren't there when he got hurt?"

"No. I only heard about it after he was in the hospital."

A little of the fire goes out of her small, dark eyes. "You really don't know, do you?" I shake my head. I have no idea what she's trying to tell me. She pauses, her upper lip trembling. With her dogs all around her, she's usually pretty scary, but right now she looks a little scared herself. "Your friend," she says. "I found him in my *yard*."

The words travel through my body like a shock wave.

Will was in the Dog Lady's yard.

The idea is so strange I can't wrap my head around it.

"I really do hope your friend gets better," she says as she tugs her dogs back onto the sidewalk and shuffles away.

I'm standing at the curb, watching her turn the corner at the end of the block when our front door flies open and Mom comes running outside in bare feet.

"He's awake!" Mom shouts. "Will's awake!"

30
CHEDDAR BABY

THE NIGHT WILL GOT hurt, the Dog Lady lied. She didn't find Will on Brookside Drive. She found him in her yard. That's why her lights went on when I ran by. She was home. As Mom drives us to the hospital, I put two and two together.

Is that why Jared didn't want me talking to the Dog Lady? Did he leave Will in her *yard*?

"He said he was going to take care of Will," I say out loud, and Mom glances over at me.

"What, honey?"

I don't know what to say. The Dog Lady was afraid her dogs were going to take the blame for Will getting hurt, so she lied about where she found him. But she didn't admit that. Not exactly. And she didn't say Jared put him there, but that must be what happened.

"Can I see Will when we get there?" I ask Mom.

"Gina said he asked for you. He's still groggy, but apparently he's very insistent that he talk to you immediately."

I swallow against the lump forming in my throat. I'm excited, I'm scared, I'm worried. What does Will remember from that night? Is he mad at me for running away?

My phone lights up with a text from Sam. "Did you talk to the Dog Lady?"

"Yes. Will's awake," I write back.

Then I tap Cal's name and write the same message.

We pull into the hospital parking lot and walk toward the visitor entrance. Mom gets a call, and I stand there while she talks, feeling more and more stressed. It's been a week since we last visited Will. Is he going to look better? Or even skinnier and grayer?

"Dad's getting Shelley from the high school," Mom says. "They'll meet us here soon."

"Okay."

I follow her inside, but it's like my feet are detached from my body. I can't feel them touching the ground, but somehow I'm moving forward, through the safety checkpoints and past the name-tag desk. This time, we take the elevator to a different floor and a different waiting area that looks exactly like the one we waited in the night Will got hurt. The chairs are stiff and there's a television flashing in the corner. I keep noticing the air-conditioning vent whirring, and sharp voices coming from the television. The fading sunlight cuts bright slashes through the blinds that bend in zigzags over the chair backs. I'm spinning my fidget ring to keep from bouncing out of the chair when I realize Will's dad is there.

"Max," Mom says with a little let's-go wave.

I jump up and shove my hands in my pockets. I don't know where else to put them.

We walk down a hall and stop outside a room with a closed door. "Just a second," Will's dad says. He disappears inside and comes out with Will's mom.

"Gina!" Mom says. They throw their arms around each other and hug.

"I can't believe it—"

"I'm so glad—"

"Such a relief—"

Will's mom pulls away with tears in her eyes but a huge smile on her face. "Max," she says to me. "Will's been asking for you, but he's still very tired. Just a few minutes, okay?"

"Okay."

I wait for Mom to come with me, but she just says, "Go on. Go see your friend."

I don't know what I'm expecting when I push through the door to Will's room, but I'm surprised to see him propped up in bed, eating a chocolate pudding cup.

"Dude," I say, and Will's head turns.

He looks paler than normal, and he has a new pair of glasses that are brown instead of blue. He smiles. "Hey, bro."

That's what we always call each other. *Bro.*

Me, Will, and Joey. The Three Broskateers.

"Want some pudding?" he says. "They gave me, like, twenty of these." He looks down to grab one and adjusts his glasses, and that one simple movement makes my heart squeeze. He hands me a pudding cup, and I sit on the bottom edge of the bed to eat it. We both scrape at our plastic cups.

"This is so weird," I say.

"I know. Was this you?" he asks, pointing at the *Minecraft* Steve bobblehead.

"Yeah."

We kind of sit there looking at each other for a minute.

"What happened at the roundhouse?" I ask, at the same moment Will says, "I'm sorry."

"Wait," I say. "Why are *you* sorry?"

Will blinks and pushes his glasses up again. "I'm sorry we went to the Res."

"So am I. I should have stopped it."

"Me too." He looks so relieved. "Mom told me I had an accident the night we went over to Joey's. I don't remember anything after being at his house."

"You don't remember going to the roundhouse?"

He shakes his head.

"Jared scared me and I took off," I say. "I'm sorry, Will."

Will shrugs. "I could have left, too, but I guess I didn't."

Joey wanted to go, and I didn't stop it, and Will didn't leave. Jared didn't do the right thing, and Luca covered it up, and the Dog Lady lied. I'm not the only one who made bad choices that night. We all did. Maybe we're all to blame for what happened to Will.

"I'm glad you're okay. I'm sure no one will notice the brain damage."

He laughs. "Remember that show we watched when

we got to Joey's, with the guy who cried over that melted cheese? I remember *that*."

"He called it his cheddar baby."

"He couldn't believe he left it out in the sun."

I'm smiling so hard my face hurts. "Imagine crying over a TV show."

"Imagine being garbage at Bed Wars," Will counters.

"Imagine being asleep for three whole weeks," a voice says from across the room.

We look up.

Joey's standing in the doorway.

31
SORRY NOT SORRY

AT FIRST, NEITHER WILL nor I say anything. Knowing what I know about the Dog Lady finding Will in her yard, I can't believe Joey would show up here.

"You got my message," Will says, and Joey nods.

I look at Will. "You asked him to come?"

"Yeah. Why wouldn't I?"

I look from Will to Joey, and Joey's got this expression on his face like he's on top of a very tall building and about to fall off.

"Want a pudding cup?" Will says, and his smile is so *real* I can't ruin it. I have to sit there while Joey eats a chocolate pudding cup and listens to Will apologize for the things he can't even remember.

"I'm sorry I wanted to go to the roundhouse," Joey says.

Which reminds me that I've heard those words from him before.

The morning we came to the hospital, me and Mom sat in the waiting room, hoping for news about Will. Different people in scrubs came in and out. A little girl lay in her dad's lap, sleeping. An old man kept coughing every few minutes, making me jump. My mind was a river of twisted-up thoughts that kept drowning me over and over again.

Every time someone came into the waiting room, I thought they were coming to give us horrible news about Will, but they always went to someone else.

All I could think was that I wanted Will to be okay. What was I supposed to do if he wasn't? When you're a kid, no one talks to you about the idea of other kids dying. It's not right that it happens, so we don't talk about it. We just sit in the waiting room and wait.

The chairs were awful. Hard wooden arms, square sides. I couldn't get comfortable. The morning news was on the TV. Mom kept humming to herself, and this one light in the corner of the waiting room kept flickering off, then turning back on again.

Start. Restart. Start. Restart.

It felt like hours later when Joey walked in with his mom. And it didn't even cross my mind that he should have been with his dad and Jared.

Joey sat next to me. "Hey."

"Hey."

He made this weird hiccupping noise. "I'm sorry I wanted to go to the roundhouse."

"Me too."

"I'm really sorry, Max."

We were the kind of friends who hugged, so I put my arm around him and we sat there feeling awful together. Joey kept shuddering. I couldn't see it then, why he was so sorry, because sometimes you see things the way you want to see them, instead of the way they really are.

Then Detective Sherman showed up, and we all took turns answering her questions.

Only some of us weren't telling the truth.

"Are you sorry you lied?" I blurt out, and Joey stops saying whatever he was in the middle of saying. I have no idea, because I had totally zoned out while my brain was reminding me of something I'd forgotten, but needed to remember.

Just like it had so many times since Will got hurt. For the first time, I think maybe Mom's right. Just because my brain works differently doesn't mean I'm broken. I'm just me, and this is how I work, and that's okay.

"What?" Will says.

Joey's silent, the way he has been so much since Will's accident.

"When Detective Sherman showed up at the hospital, you kept telling her that Will went after me when you knew he didn't." My voice catches. "How could you do that?"

Joey moves off the bed. "I should go."

"Does it matter?" Will says, because that's the kind of person Will is. He apologizes when he burps. He offers you his sandwich before you can twist his arm to swap. He never wants me or Joey to be mad at him, so he always does whatever we want. Even when it hurts him.

"Did you leave Will in the Dog Lady's yard?" I say to Joey. "That's where she says she found him."

Joey's eyes go wide. "She found him in her *yard*?" he says. For a second, it looks like he's about to come clean. Then he turns and runs out of the room.

32
TRAPPED

FOR A SPLIT SECOND after Joey runs out of the room, I'm frozen. Will looks at me in total confusion. "What did you just say about the Dog Lady's yard?"

"I'll explain it later." I fling the door open and tear down the hall after Joey.

"Young man, slow down!" someone shouts, but I don't even see who, I'm moving so fast. When I burst into the waiting area, a whole bunch of faces look at me in surprise. Mom, Dad, Shelley. Will's mom and dad. And Sam. She's here with her dad.

"Which way did he go?" I ask, panting.

"Down the stairs," Sam says, because she gets me.

And I get her.

I run for the door to the stairs and fling it open. Dad

shouts, "Max!" but I have to keep going or I won't be able to catch up. Joey's a lot faster than me. I take the stairs two at a time, swinging my body over the landings with the handrails until I get to the ground floor. There's no sign of Joey in the lobby, but the big double doors are right there.

I burst outside into the dusky parking lot.

"Joey!" I shout.

Two heads turn my way. Jared and Mr. Peterson are standing next to Mr. Peterson's truck. Across the parking lot, a flash of light blond hair appears between two cars.

I take off running.

Mr. Peterson shouts something after me, and I hear car doors slamming, but I'm trying to keep going as fast as I can. Joey crosses the street toward downtown, and I sprint after him, jumping between people and lampposts and dodging benches as the sun goes down behind me. I think he's headed for the arcade, but then he turns right, toward the middle school. Which makes sense. Joey always likes to hang out there after school.

My phone blows up in my pocket, and I manage to fish it out while I'm running.

"Dad!"

"Sam filled me in," he says. "Where are you?"

"I think—Joey's going—to the middle school," I manage to say between pants.

"We're on our way," Dad says, and hangs up before I can ask who "we" is. I stuff my phone back in my pocket. I'm just trying to survive the longest sprint of my life without splitting in two. I've never been good at distance running, and right now it feels like my liver's exploding. The cramp is so bad it has me clutching my ribs and wheezing as I jog into the middle school parking lot and squint into the darkness behind the building.

"Joey!" I shout.

There's no answer, but I hear the unmistakable sound of a metal door handle being pumped. I half run, half limp into the little vestibule at the back of the building that leads to the rear doors. Joey's in the dark recess, facing the doors, pressing the bar and getting nowhere.

"They're locked," I say. It's getting late, and no one's at school anymore. "*Joey*," I shout, and he finally turns around.

His face is streaked with tears. "Just leave me alone."

"I can't do that," I say, as I bend over my knees and pray for the side cramp to end. Our chests are both heaving. The air fills with the sound of our panting.

Joey looks left and right. He tries to run past me, but

I spread my arms, blocking the entrance to the vestibule. "Come on, man. Just stop it."

His shoulders slump.

He's trapped. There's nowhere to go but the truth.

"Did you guys dump Will in the Dog Lady's yard?"

"No!"

"Well, that's where she found him. How do you explain that?"

"Jared said he was taking care of Will," Joey says. He clenches his shaggy blond hair. His chest heaves with a sob. He looks up at me, his blue eyes bright with tears. "Will was in the Dog Lady's *yard*?"

"Yeah."

Joey's whole face crumbles. "I can't believe he did that."

"Who? Jared?" I wait, but Joey doesn't say anything. "Come on, man. How else did Will end up with the Dog Lady? Either Jared left Will in her yard or he left Will lying by the side of the road, and both of those are awful. So which one is it? What happened that night?"

"I don't know!" Joey shouts. "Jared said he worked something out, and I just thought, I don't know—I thought he made a deal with her or something."

"Are you kidding me?"

"It was an accident!"

"I know! And it would've been okay if you had just done the right thing. No one made you guys lie about this. All you had to do was be honest."

"I didn't have a choice."

I take a step toward him. "That's bull and you know it. You can be honest now."

"Why do you even care?" he says. "Will's okay. He woke up."

"Because! I want *us* back," I shout, and as soon as the words leave my lips, I realize how true they are. If Joey doesn't come clean, we'll never be friends again.

Nothing will ever be okay unless we make this right.

"Look," I say, raising my hands the way Cal always did. "I messed up this summer. I'm sorry. I didn't mean to forget about you, but I did, and that sucks."

Joey's chest heaves.

"It's time for you to show up for Will. That's what a real friend does. You tell the truth."

Joey nods miserably. "Jared's going to kill me," he says. "My dad, too."

"Yeah, but Will needs you."

"I know. I'm sorry," he says, and for a second, I think

we're going to turn this whole thing around. Joey will tell the police what he knows, and Will's parents will finally have the answers they deserve, and we can all get past this.

The Three Broskateers can live to game another day.

Then I hear an engine approach behind me, and headlights cut through the darkness of the vestibule. I turn around, blocking the light with my arm, but the headlights stay on. Two dark figures cut in front of the glare.

"There you are," a deep voice says as Mr. Peterson and Jared step into view.

And then we're both trapped.

33
SLOW MOTION

TIME SLOWS DOWN WHEN bad things happen. I remember how long that run through the woods was, the night we went into the Res. It felt like I would never see the house lights again. It's always right before you give up that you finally get there.

When I see Jared and Mr. Peterson, I want to run. My muscles even brace for takeoff, and my heart starts racing, the walls of my chest going thick and heavy.

Then I hear Joey sniffle behind me, and I know I'm not going anywhere.

Not without him.

"I know what happened to Will," I say, and Mr. Peterson frowns.

He looks past me. "What did you do?" he asks Joey.

"He already knew," Joey says. "Please don't be mad."

"The Dog Lady told me she found Will in her yard." I look at Jared, and he has the decency to drop his chin in shame.

"You said you took care of him," Joey says, and Jared rubs a hand over his face.

"I'm sorry," Jared mutters.

Mr. Peterson shakes his head. "Will is fine."

"He's not fine," I say, and Mr. Peterson fixes his hot gaze on me. "Will's in the hospital. He's skinny and tired, and he doesn't even remember what happened."

"That's enough," Mr. Peterson says.

"We all went into the woods that night, and we shouldn't have." I look at Jared again. "You know it, and Joey knows it. What happened is all our faults. But you're the one who dumped Will in the Dog Lady's backyard. *You* did that."

Mr. Peterson has gone very still. "If you know what's best for you, you'll stop running your mouth right this second. What's done is done. Let's just move on."

"Wait. Did you know what Jared did?" Joey asks.

"He helped me," Jared says.

"That's *enough*," Mr. Peterson says. "Come on, Joey. Let's go." He's breathing hard. The air fills his chest like a barrel. He takes a step toward us, but Jared cuts in front of him.

"It's over, Dad," Jared says. "I'm done lying."

"I did this to keep you out of trouble," Mr. Peterson says, but Jared stands firm.

"The kid's right," Jared says. "We didn't hurt Will, but we didn't help him, either. That's on us." He looks over his shoulder at me and Joey. "I'm sorry I lied."

"You're going to ruin your whole future over this?" Mr. Peterson says.

"What about Will's future?" I shout, and he glares at me.

"I didn't do anything wrong," Jared says to his father. "Not until I listened to *you*."

"We're done here," Mr. Peterson says. He points at the truck. "Get in. *Now*."

Jared flinches, and for a second, I can see it. How we all go in circles. How things repeat. How those patterns make us who we are. But maybe we don't have to follow those patterns. Maybe we can change them.

I pat my pocket. My phone is right where it should be. "Stop!" I shout, while I turn the camera on and hit the red button. Mr. Peterson freezes, realizing that he's being recorded.

Then there's a honking sound I will never forget.

The supervan comes roaring across the parking lot and hops the curb, coming to a lurching stop in front of the vestibule. The van hasn't even stopped rocking when Cal leaps down from the driver's seat. He jogs over and gets in front of us with his hands up.

"Let's all take it down a notch, shall we?" he says.

Mr. Peterson takes a step back.

Dad appears from the other side of the supervan. "It's over, Frank," he says. "You've got to do the right thing by your kids. Let us help you."

For a second, Mr. Peterson looks as if he's about to take a swing at Dad or Cal, but then all the fight drains out of his body. His hands fall limp at his sides.

Blue and red lights flash in the background.

"It's over," Dad repeats. He puts a hand on Mr. Peterson's shoulder and leads him aside.

Cal comes over to me and Joey. "You boys okay?" He squeezes my shoulder, and I throw my arms around him. He stumbles back, laughing a little.

"You came back," I say through the tightness in my throat.

"I'm sorry, kiddo," he says. "I never should have left."

34
BYE FOR NOW

CAL PILES ANOTHER SLICE of roasted chicken on his plate. Dad decided that what we needed after all the excitement this week was a huge meal. It's Friday night, and he's whipped up a roasted chicken, baked sweet potatoes, green beans with butter and garlic, and fluffy yeast rolls from dough he made himself. Now it's almost dark out, and we're all stuffed.

Cal leans back in his chair and groans. "You're gonna ruin me, Tim."

"Can't have you hitting the road hungry," Dad jokes, but his eyes are sad.

Cal's heading back to Arizona tomorrow. That's the deal he made with his parole officer, after Detective Sherman said Cal had been extremely helpful in resolving Will

Schwartz's case. It's Cal's first parole violation, so there's wiggle room as long as he gets back by next week.

"I wish you didn't have to leave," I say.

"I know, buddy."

Mom wipes a stray tear from her cheek. "Stop it, or I'm going to start crying again."

Cal looks a little weepy himself. "I'm sorry I wasn't around the last couple of years, Em."

"It's fine," she says with a watery smile, but this is the good kind of fine, because they are finally on the same page. "You'll let me know how your appointment with Dr. Levine goes?"

"Of course."

We've been talking about ADHD a lot this past week. Cal and Mom are both getting tested. Dr. W helped Cal find a therapist in Arizona, now that he's really leaving. Turns out, he only made it as far as the ancient, red-roofed motel by the highway on Sunday. He got to the on-ramp and couldn't make himself take it. He said he couldn't leave, not without saying goodbye.

It was just good timing that Cal came back when I texted him. He showed up at the hospital right after I ran off, and he and Dad jumped right back in the supervan to find me. After the police arrived, we all gave our statements, and Joey's mom came to take Jared and Joey home. They're staying with her for now, until Mr. Peterson completes counseling and parenting classes, or whatever else the family court says he has to do to prove he can be trusted again.

Will's accident has been ruled just that—an accident—but that's no excuse for not doing the right thing. Jared and Joey are doing counseling, too, so now we have that in common. Dr. W said it's going to be a process fixing things with Joey, but that's normal. There's no such thing as perfect. There's only trying, and sometimes failing, and that's okay.

Shelley tings the side of her glass with her fork. "I'd like to propose a toast," she says, and we all grab our glasses. "To Dad, for absolutely crushing this meal."

We all clink our glasses and Dad laughs. "Thanks. It was my pleasure."

"You know what you need?" Cal says. "A hobby. You should take up woodworking."

Mom smiles. "Tim won't have much time for hobbies anymore. Tell them, honey."

Dad clears his throat. "One of the companies I pitched the granola to has invited me to join their development team to create a new line of snack products."

Mom squeals and claps.

"Go, Dad!" Shelley says, while I give him a high five.

Cal claps Dad on the back. "That is aces, man. They couldn't have picked a better guy."

"Just wait until you try the tomato-basil popcorn I'm working on first," Dad says.

Cal groans. "Do I have to?"

Mom laughs. "Yes," she says, her face going fake serious. "As a card-carrying member of this family, you are obligated to eat strange popcorn."

"Hey!" Dad says.

"I like popcorn," I say, and Dad points at me.

"See now, that's more like it," he says.

We all laugh.

"What are you gonna do without us around to bug you anymore?" Cal asks Mom.

Mom looks a little sheepish. "Actually, it might be time for me to take a little break from real estate. I've been considering going back to school to finish my degree."

"You totally should," Shelley says.

"Ooh! You and mom can go to college *together*," I say, and Shelley's face goes still.

"Wait," she says. "That's a horrible idea."

"No take backs," I say.

"Imagine listening to your little brother," Shelley says, and I crack up.

This time it's Mom who taps the side of her water glass. "A toast," she says. "To family."

We raise our glasses. "To family!"

The next morning, the supervan is packed to the ceiling with enough supplies to sustain a small army for a week, instead of Cal for the three days it will take him to drive back to Arizona.

"There's still time to squeeze in there," Cal jokes as Sam and I stare at the wall of supplies Mom has built at the back of the van.

"I'll never fit."

He laughs. "I know, kiddo."

Sam hands Cal the bakery box she brought with her this afternoon. "Well, you have to find room for this. They're the best pastries in all of New Jersey."

"That, I can do," Cal says. "Thank you."

"See you later, funcle," Sam says. She squeezes my hand and heads back into the house. We're working on a new writing project together. This one has her words and my drawings, and it's going to be amazing. After the truth came out about Will, Sam told her parents about everything we'd done. They get it now, about her being a journalist. They're okay with her working a little less at the bakery so she has time for the school newspaper, too. Earlier in the week, we went over to Bovella's and saw the new display cases. They looked perfect. Like they had always been there, but better. Cal says it's the history in the wood.

"You can fake a lot of things, but you can't fake history," he said.

Cal shuts the van's rear doors and latches them tight.

He's leaving in just a few minutes.

I don't know how I'm going to say goodbye.

Will is coming home this afternoon. His parents bought him a bunk bed, and me and Cal helped them put it together this week. Will's parents never let him have a bunk bed before even though he begged for one, because he didn't have a sibling, but now they say there's no excuse. As Cal says, we have to live life to the fullest because we never know when the ride might be over. I can't wait to build a fort with Will, and to go back to Yestercades with Will and Joey, once Will can play video games again.

I follow Cal to the front of the van. He's already said goodbye to the rest of the family. I think Mom is giving me this time because she knows how much he means to me.

She knew it before I did.

Cal opens the driver's door and my throat tightens. "Remember to check your blind spots," I joke.

He laughs. "I will."

Then he wraps me in a big bear hug. I've started collecting our adventures in my writer's notebook. The pages are a mash-up between graphic novel and prose, which Ms. Little says is exciting. According to her, the rules of writing are more like suggestions. They're meant to be broken. The key is knowing when to take your own path. She says I'm getting there.

Cal wipes at his eyes. I'm sniffling, too.

"It's not goodbye forever," he says into my ear. "Just bye for now." He gives me one last squeeze and lets me go. "I'll talk to you soon, kid. Call me anytime."

"I will."

He climbs in and shuts the door. The engine roars to life. His arm hangs out the busted window. "Be good, Max," he says. "I gotta go see about a girl."

"Thanks for being on my team!" I shout over the engine.

He grins. "Always."

The supervan pulls away from the curb.

Turns the corner.

And he's gone.

35
TAKE TWO

I'VE BEEN THINKING ABOUT that letter I wrote at the beginning of the school year to my future self, and how I want to change it now. Ms. Little says that's a great idea. I can do as many drafts as I need.

"Writing is rewriting," she says. "Give me your revision anytime you like."

Dear Max,

By the time you read this letter you will be finished with sixth grade. I hope it got easier. It started out hard. Congratulations on surviving one year of middle school!

What is next year like? Are you over six feet tall now? How many writer's notebooks did you use? My guess is three. Did you like Arizona? Mom says we're going there for Thanksgiving. I'm sure they have turkeys in Arizona, but it will be hot, so Dad says we might make tacos instead.

I hope you finished the graphic novel you're writing, and if you didn't, there's always next year. Ms. Little says all books are written one word at a time, but maybe you can invent a robot to write it all at once. ☺

I hope you're still friends with Joey and Will, and that Sam isn't sick of arguing with you yet. I bet the rest of the year was good, but if anything else went wrong, it's okay. No one's perfect. Everyone makes mistakes.

Stay weird,
Max

ACKNOWLEDGMENTS

Attention-deficit/hyperactivity disorder (ADHD) is a condition that includes difficulties with attention, increased activity, and difficulties with impulsivity. Estimates show that 11 percent of school-aged children and about 4 percent of adults have ADHD. It is usually first identified when children are school-aged, although it also can be diagnosed in people of all age groups. In an average classroom of thirty children, research suggests that at least one student will have ADHD.*

My personal experience with ADHD began when I met a boy in high school who would later become my husband. As teenagers, I watched him struggle with an academic system that made no room for his way of thinking. He was brilliant, but the system was inflexible and often unkind. Since then, a lot has changed. Today, children with ADHD are often recognized, and support services and accommodations are available, which I've navigated as the parent of a child with ADHD in public school. I'm grateful to the

---

* Opening statistics cited from CHADD

countless educators who make a place for everyone in their classrooms, but more work remains to be done.

I owe a debt of gratitude to the many experts who discussed this story with me and helped me portray Max and his family to the best of my ability. Any faults that persist are mine and mine alone. Thank you to Rebekah Cianci, LPC, Board Certified Behavioral Analyst; Brooks Benjamin, certified teacher and librarian, Cherokee Middle School; Paul Adams, special education teacher, Essex High School; Becky Appleby-Sparrow; Rhonda Battenfelder; Lindsay Eagar; Ella Schwartz; George Iannuzzi, English teacher, Chatham Middle School; Sarah Pasternak, English teacher, Chatham Middle School; Oona Marie Abrams, English teacher, Chatham High School; Mindy Fliegelman, fourth-grade teacher, Whittier Elementary School; Maudjah Henriquez-Francis, school counselor; Dr. Laurie B. Levine, PhD; Marisa White, vice principal of North Johnston Middle School. Credit for the Story Spine concept goes to playwright Kenn Adams.

Thank you to Liz Kossnar for being so supportive and fun to work with! We make a pretty great team. Thank you also to Aria Balraj, Siena Koncsol, Victoria Stapleton, Andrea Cruise, Amber Mercado, Christie Michel, and the entire Little, Brown Books for Young Readers team.

Thank you to Elena Giovinazzo for being a true dream agent and to Holly McGhee, Ashley Valentine, Cameron Chase, and everyone at Pippin Properties, Inc.

In the unpredictable world of publishing, my writing friends are indispensable. Thank you for always being there, Laura Shovan, Lois Sepahban, Tracey Baptiste, Lindsay Eagar, Paula Chase, Sabrina Bailey, Martha Brockenbrough (and Lucy Berliant), #MGbetareaders, Fight Me Club. Thank you also to Words Bookstore in Maplewood, New Jersey; Scuppernong Books in Greensboro, North Carolina; the South Orange Public Library; and Keisha Miller. All my love to my Novel Bites: Barbara, Michelle, Christine (and Imy!), Bridget, Melissa, Romaine (my namesake for Dr. W), and Leána.

To my family: Thank you for always being there. Mom, I promise I'll get Rose in the next book. Dad, thanks for getting through the tough moments this year. Ris, thank you for always answering all my questions. Thanks for the support, Maggie and Rich and all the extended Conklin family. Brandt, thank you for being the inspiration for Max's height in this story—keep being awesome.

To Andrew: Thank you for tolerating endless questions and for being so patient with me. Perry, thank you for all the insights and jokes. Alec, thank you for being my number one fan—I really depend on those sales! ☺ Charlotte, thank you for being the best writing assistant ever.

The soundtrack for writing this book included: "Shadow of the Day" by Linkin Park, "Experience" by Ludovico Einaudi, "Welcome Home, Son" by Radical Face, "I Miss You" by blink-182, "Screen" by Twenty One Pilots, "Agnes" by

Glass Animals, "Little Lion Man" by Mumford & Sons, "Hot Pink Lighter" by Cold Hart and YAWNS, "Figure It Out" by Chaos Chaos, "Song for Zula" by Phosphorescent, "Wiseblood" by Zola Jesus and Johnny Jewel, and "Demons" by Imagine Dragons, among others.

If ADHD symptoms are causing problems for you or your child, please know that federal law requires schools to provide equal education opportunities to students with disabilities under Section 504, and you can find more information in the *Know Your Rights: Students with ADHD* guide from the U.S. Department of Education's Office for Civil Rights. All individuals are protected by the Americans with Disabilities Act (ADA) and the Americans with Disabilities Act Amendments Act (ADAAA) of 2008, and if you need help navigating workplace accommodations, the Job Accommodation Network (JAN) can help at askjan.org.

In the course of writing this book, I consulted many texts and organizations that readers may find helpful, including Children and Adults with Attention-Deficit/Hyperactivity Disorder (CHADD); the *ADHD reWired* podcast by Eric Tivers; the *Black Girl Lost Keys* blog by René Brooks; the Distraction series by Dr. Edward Hallowell, MD; Attention Deficit Disorder Association (ADDA); *ADDitude* magazine; and *Taking Charge of ADHD: The Complete, Authoritative Guide for Parents* by Russell A. Barkley, PhD.

To all my readers: I believe in you. Write your own manual!